Mail Order Bride : Miriam's Story

Sarah Amberson

Published by Trellis Publishing, 2021.

This is a work of fiction. Similarities to real people, places, or events are entirely coincidental.

MAIL ORDER BRIDE : MIRIAM'S STORY

First edition. June 29, 2021.

Copyright © 2021 Sarah Amberson.

ISBN: 979-8224364879

Written by Sarah Amberson.

MAIL ORDER BRIDE : MIRIAM'S STORY

SARAH AMBERSON

The smile on Miriam's face didn't feel right. She knew that it was right, but she couldn't help but feel she was betraying herself. She never knew this was where she would end up, marrying for a second time at twenty-five years old and for necessity instead of love.

She gave a guarded look over to Fredrick. He was tall and handsome enough, but she didn't love him. She didn't know anything about him besides his name and where he lived. Miriam sighed. She couldn't go back now.

"Miriam, do you take Fredrick to be your lawfully wedded husband?" The justice of the peace's voice interrupted her sad thoughts.

Miriam only hesitated for a second. She clenched her light blue day dress a little tighter and managed a soft, "I do." She didn't hear the rest of the ceremony, but soon she had a ring on her finger and was riding beside Fredrick in the wagon towards his ranch.

She'd only been in town for a day and hadn't been to his ranch. The ride was beautiful in its own way. The setting sun reminded her that the last chapter of her life was closed forever. Even though that was a good thing she couldn't help but feel the sadness come over her once again.

The wagon stopped in front of a modest ranch house.

"Is this it?" She tried to sound excited.

"No, we're picking up my daughter." Fredrick said gruffly as he leapt down from the wagon seat. When he didn't ask her to join him, Miriam stayed seated. She had wondered where Leah was. She had been mentioned quite a few times in their correspondence. Now that she was about to meet her, Miriam felt a flutter of nervousness.

As Leah came from the house clutching her father's hand tightly, with her little cheeks flushed red, memories hit Miriam like bricks and she had to keep the tears from coming to her eyes. In her other hand she clutched a stuffed dog whose long ears were worn from being carried by them. One black button eye was missing.

Fredrick pushed Leah forward. "Say hello, Leah." He urged.

"Hello," she said, so softly that Miriam could hardly hear her. Leah looked at the ground sadly and only glanced up for a second. After the awkward introductions were over Leah was seated comfortably in the back of the wagon and they continued their silent ride until they arrived at Fredrick's ranch.

Miriam wasn't sure what she had expected when she had made the decision to move to Wyoming, but she was sure she had her fair share of challenges ahead.

As the horse trotted on, her mind wandered, and she played the scene that seemed to never end again in her mind. She wondered if she could ever forget, if she could ever find peace from the past that forever haunted her.

"Mama, can me and Clair go buy some candy?" Becky tugged at Miriam's hand. Miriam looked back down at her daughter's clear blue eyes. For five years old, she was very independent.

"I suppose, but hurry," she conceded reluctantly. On one hand, she didn't like the two little girls to go off shopping on their own, but then again, the candy store was just a couple of houses down the street.

Clair's mother, Jenny smiled at them as they went. "They grow up so fast," she sighed sadly.

"Yes, they do," Miriam said, watching the two little girls hop and skip towards the candy store, warm pennies clutched in their hands.

They didn't come to town often, maybe once every two weeks, and Becky enjoyed it just as much as Miriam did.

"My hen stopped sitting again, she just up and left all her eggs. By the time I noticed it was too late to save any," Miriam said, frustrated. It was the third time this had happened, and Miriam was getting fed up with losing so many little chicks.

"Oh, I'm sorry. I have a sitter I can lend you if you'd like. Good ones are so hard to come by," Clair's mother clucked sympathetically. "My dear husband's family came calling this last month," she added with an annoyed look. "I do believe they don't like me."

Miriam laughed. "I'm sure there's something about you that they like," she consoled her friend. "Everyone has problems with family at one moment or another."

Suddenly a loud commotion caught both of their attention. A horse and wagon came barreling down Main Street. The driver was pulling at the reigns, calling for help, but all could tell he was no match for the out-of-control beasts.

Then a sight caught Miriam's eye that stopped her cold. Clair and Betty were in the street chasing a piece of paper that danced in the wind ahead of them.

"Becky!" Miriam frantically called out. Her feet were already moving. She knew she wasn't going to get there in time.

There was a scream and a flash of grey as Becky in her little grey dress disappeared underneath the wagon.

Claire had fallen just out of reach of the runaway wagon and now stood open mouthed, watching as Miriam raced to Becky's side. She lay in the middle of the dusty road, tears streaming down her now white face.

"I didn't see them mama! I'm sorry," Clair sobbed.

"It's okay. It's okay." Jenny stroked her hair gently.

Moments later, someone had called the doctor and he knelt caringly beside Becky. He checked her over carefully and then turned to Miriam. He shook his head gravely and desperation washed over the terrified mother.

"Is she going to be okay?" She asked loudly. Looking back at Becky she saw her eyes were beginning to close.

"Mama I'm so tired." Becky said weakly.

"No honey, please don't go to sleep," she begged her daughter as she clutched her tiny hand.

Becky's eyes closed, and her breathing slowed. "It hurts, Mama," she whispered.

"Please do something!" Miriam pleaded, but the doctor shook his head and looked at her with sympathy in his eyes.

"I'm sorry, Miriam. But there's nothing I can do."

Miriam gathered her daughter into her arms and rocked back and forth. "I love you, baby," she said through her sobs. She knew that she was gone. She would never see her sweet Becky again.

Fredrick set the last of Miriam's suitcases in her room. He had noticed she seemed as uncomfortable at their union as he had. He couldn't say that he had even seen himself getting wed yet again, but here he was.

He shook his head. He wasn't getting attached this time. Last time it had nearly been the undoing of him and if it hadn't been for Leah he never would've remarried. Poor little Leah, he couldn't let her suffer because of his and Kitty's decisions.

At the thought of Kitty, a foul taste filled his mouth.

"The house is lovely." Miriam's gentle voice interrupted his thoughts.

"Glad you like it." He said curtly. He didn't care if she liked the house or not. He cared more about whether she got along with Leah or not, but so far, Leah could barely say hello.

Sighing, he realized it was going to take some weeks of patience to get the two used to each other. He didn't need the extra work, he had enough work trying to recuperate the ranch after his months of absence.

"Shall I start some dinner?" It was Miriam again, and Fredrick found himself almost annoyed by her. Couldn't she tell that no one else was here to do it?

"That would be good," he said, and by the flash of hurt that passed through her eyes he knew he'd been a little too gruff.

"Leah, go help Miriam with dinner." He pushed his shy six-year-old daughter towards Miriam who was looking at her a little wistfully. Leah went as she had been bidden, but she looked as if she was afraid Miriam was going to make her for dinner.

Fredrick felt defeated as he went out to milk the cows. He was now married to a girl with seemingly little initiative and he had a clingy child, who so far, didn't seem to like her new mother. He wasn't sure he liked her either. Making his way towards his evening chores he tuned his thoughts out and focused on his work. He couldn't afford distractions.

—-*—-

"Darling I'm home!" Fredrick called out gleefully. He held a wildflower he'd found down by the river behind his back. Kitty was a city girl, but she did have the odd appreciation for his gestures, even when they were simple and small.

Silence greeted him.

"Leah? Kitty?" Still nothing. A hint of worry tugged at the back of his mind as he began to search the house. The simple ranch house he'd built with his own hands wasn't that large. It consisted of a kitchen, fireplace living area, and three bedrooms.

At the last bedroom he heard a soft crying. Bursting in he was surprised to find four-year-old Leah curled up in the corner of her bed sobbing her eyes out into her arms.

"Leah? Where's mama?" Fredrick asked a little urgently. The feeling that something was wrong was growing with every minute.

"Sh- she's gone," the little girl wailed.

"What do you mean she's gone?" Fredrick felt his heart beating harder and harder. What was Leah talking about? Maybe she didn't know...

"She left, and she said she's never coming back! She said this was for you." She extended a small, folded, tear-stained sheet of paper towards him.

Fredrick snatched it up and began to read.

My Dearest Fredrick,

I don't expect you to understand, but I'm not happy here with you.

I've tried, I really have, but I just can't be a country girl. I miss the

city. I miss my friends. I'm not ready to be a wife. I'm not ready to be a

mother. I never meant to hurt you and Leah. Please try to understand.

- Yours,

Kitty

The air fled from Fredrick's lungs. Kitty had always been a city girl, but Fredrick had hoped that in time she could learn to love the country. She had often mentioned how she wanted to visit her friends in the city or how she wished they would bring a moving picture to their town someday, but how had he not seen that she was so unhappy? Where had she gone? Maybe he could find her. And how could she leave her child?

"Oh honey, there must be a mistake. I can't believe she would leave forever," he tried to console the child even though in his heart he feared it might really be true that she had gone forever.

Scooping Leah up he wrapped a blanket around her and rushed out to the front where his horse was still tethered. Mounting quickly, he wasted no time in dropping Leah off with their friends at a neighboring homestead, and then rode in the direction of town.

When he got there he saw no sign of Kitty. He ran towards the post office. Stage coaches always passed by the post office, maybe they would know something.

"Have you seen Kitty?" He gasped out through heavy breaths. The large man attending the window gave him a look of pity.

"You've missed her by a couple of hours. She left on the stage coach this afternoon." The man looked at Fredrick sadly. "I'm sorry."

Fredrick stared off into the horizon. He'd lost her. He was too late.

It had been a year since Kitty had left. Fredrick downed yet another glass of alcohol. The saloon had been a regular stop for him since Kitty had taken off. Some days he woke and expected to see her there cooking breakfast.

Leah still cried at night and asked for mama and he couldn't get Kitty out of his thoughts. Was she doing okay? Where had she gone? Was she happy? What had he done wrong? Would she ever return?

Angrily he stood from the table, he hadn't planted the ranch or worked on adding a room or any of his other projects. He just couldn't find the energy. He needed to do something to get his family back on track, or at least what was left of it.

—-*—-

Miriam hummed a familiar song as she swept her broom back and forth over the hard, wooden floor. She had completely cleaned the entire house every day since she'd arrived. It was more for herself rather than for the house.

Fredrick had made his appearances only at dinner and Miriam was finding it more and more discouraging. Between his unfriendliness and Leah's shyness she was beginning to feel downright lonely.

A small noise caused her to look to the corner of the hallway. Leah's little brown head was peeking curiously around it. Fredrick had been gone since sunrise and the little girl must have gotten tired of playing on her own.

Miriam ignored her. She remembered the way she used to try to insist Becky say hello to visitors or to her grandparents who she almost never saw. It was always so much easier when the visitors would wait for Becky to say hello to them in her own time.

After ten minutes Miriam could hardly contain her curiosity, but she stuck to it. If Leah needed something she had to ask. She really needed to learn to trust her sometime.

"Miriam?" The little voice made Miriam's heart leap.

"Yes Leah?" This time, Miriam turned her head towards. Leah who had come out from hiding and stood a couple of feet away.

"Do you want to play hide and seek with me?" She said shyly.

Miriam felt a surge of joy. Finally, Leah was going to give her a chance.

"Sure, honey. You go hide, and I'll count first." She set her broom against the wall and made a big show of not looking while listening to Leah's small feet scamper away.

As she counted to forty she remembered a how she had played hide and seek with her daughter, Becky, before the accident. Becky had been a little odd. She had always preferred searching to hiding and she remembered how thrilled she was each time she found her mother. She thought for a second how much Becky and Leah would have liked each other.

"Ready or not here I come!" She called out in warning as she shook her head in dismay.

If Becky could be here, she wouldn't be here She'd still be back in her home town with John and Becky. Miriam pushed back the tears that were forming in her eyes and went off to find Leah. This was not a time to think sad thoughts. She needed to focus on her new family.

—-*—-

Fredrick burst in through the door. He was carrying a huge load of firewood and could hardly see where he was going. Surprisingly, a gentle touch on his arm led him towards the wood box. He squashed the warm thank you that began to form in his mind and instead he dropped the wood in the box and washed his hands for dinner.

Leah was already seated and had a beautiful glow about her. She almost looked happy. Fredrick felt a flutter of hope. Maybe the two were learning to love each other after all. It had only been two months, but maybe there was a chance they would be ok.

Miriam set a plate of roast beef and potatoes in front of him. His stomach growled in hunger, but his mind was saying something else.

"This again? We've had this for two nights in a row." He grumbled in ungratefulness. He missed variety. Kitty had always taken the wagon into town and gotten what she needed to keep the kitchen stocked as well as tended the garden out back.

A nagging voice in his head told him that maybe Miriam didn't know it was okay for her to do those things. He looked up at her and was surprised to see the hurt in her eyes.

"I'm sorry, I'm sure it's great." He half apologized.

"Feel free to take the wagon and get some things from town any time. There's also a small kitchen garden out back where the vegetables are nearly ready for harvest." He instructed as he took his first bite.

As the other instances of the dish, it was quite tasty.

"Miriam and me played hide and seek today, Pa." Leah said, a sparkle in her eyes.

"It's Miriam and I." he corrected with a small smile, but he didn't miss the disappointment in Leah's eyes at his short response.

Scolding himself, he hurried with his meal. It seemed he couldn't do anything right by anyone tonight.

—-*—-

"It's your fault you know!" Miriam balked as her husband yelled the words, the words she thought she would never hear.

"How is it my fault? Do you think I wanted... that I wanted that to happen?" Miriam's voice broke and a stray tear streamed down her face.

"You always insisted on taking Becky to town with you and letting her run everywhere like she was so much older. She was five years old for goodness sakes!" Her husband's voice was louder now, and she had to keep from flinching.

"I can't even stand to look at you, knowing what you let happen!"

Miriam fought to keep control over her voice, her emotions, everything she was thinking.

"I am so sorry for what happened to Becky. I loved her so much. I have lost everything just like you," she said softly.

"You weren't careful with our daughter, Miriam. You didn't protect her. How can I forgive you for that?" he yelled before storming out of the house.

Miriam stood where he had left her, in the middle of the room. Her whole body was shaking, and she felt such despair. First, she had lost her daughter and now she was losing her husband. How could everything disappear so fast?

Miriam found herself crying silently in bed. How could she have ended up in yet another dissolving marriage? Her new husband's sleeping form loomed in the dark on the other side of the bed. He hadn't said much of anything else the whole evening. All Miriam could remember were his harsh words at dinner and Leah's crestfallen look when he'd had no interest in their games of the day.

That was probably what had hurt the most. She had realized that Fredrick had no interest in having a wife, but he had brought her here to be a mother to Leah. Didn't he care about her happiness?

Pushing the quilts gently off, she padded over to the window. It looked over the back yard into the henhouse. Everything was beautifully illuminated by the moon and Miriam could see almost all the details she could see in the daytime. The entire yard seemed to glow with the mysterious light.

"You're going to catch a cold." Fredrick's gruff voice made her jump.

"What are you looking at?" His voice was slightly kinder this time.

"Just the night. It's very pretty in the moonlight."

Not wanting keep Fredrick up any longer she made her way back to bed and lay there staring at the ceiling. Fredrick didn't say anything else and neither did she. Soon she was drifting off to sleep.

Miriam was up early the next morning but not before Fredrick. By the time she woke up he was gone. She went about the day as if it didn't bother her. She made a simple breakfast for herself and Leah and then hooked the horse up to the wagon. Soon they were riding into town. Leah had changed since the day before and was now shyly telling Miriam about school and the projects they were working on.

Miriam found her childish chatter a welcome distraction from her problems. When the got to the general store they made their way through each isle picking out the things Miriam thought they would need for a little more variety. Fredrick had left a small pile of bills on the table for her to use that morning.

"Leah honey? Is that you?" A sugary voice caused Miriam to come to a halt. A tall woman stood a few feet away. She had red blonde hair that was swept into a bun. She wore a delicate yellow day dress that was borderline white. Miriam couldn't help but think that she was absolutely beautiful.

"Mama?" Leah's uncertainty was palpable.

"That's your mother?" Miriam said uncertainly looking from the six-year-old girl to the woman staring oddly at her.

"I'm Kitty. And yes, I'm Leah's mother." The woman's tone was frosty and cold. As she reached out to take Leah's hand, Leah shrunk back against Miriam and buried her face in her skirt.

"And who are you, might I ask?" Kitty stared down at Miriam as if there was something spilled all over the front of her dress.

"I'm married to Leah's father." Miriam hoped her voice didn't waver. She wasn't about to tell this woman that she and Fredrick didn't exactly get along or that Leah had just started talking to her.

"So, he remarried." Kitty scoffed, "I should have figured. He never could take care of the child himself."

Kitty stood there for a moment, seemingly upraising Miriam. "You can leave Leah here with me," she said with a tone of finality. "I'll explain everything to Fredrick this evening."

Miriam felt her heart quicken a bit. "I won't be leaving Leah here. She is under my care. You will have to talk to Fredrick about taking her with you," Miriam responded, quite taken aback.

The woman's eye's narrowed, "I don't know who you think you are, but I'm her mother." She said harshly.

"That may be so, but I'm not just leaving her here with you. You left her, remember? Good day ma'am." Miriam turned around and pulled a confused Leah behind her. Shakily she paid for the purchases and carried them to the wagon.

Leah looked pale and frightened as if she had seen a ghost. She whimpered a little and clung to Miriam's skirt. If she had seemed shy before it seemed to have evaporated in the store. Miriam's heart went out to the little girl. Poor thing. How confusing this must be for her.

Miriam found herself shaking the entire way home. She hadn't known exactly what had happened between Fredrick and Leah's mother but now that she'd seen the woman, she knew she could lose everything. How could this woman abandon her child and husband and then just come back two years later, expecting to walk back into their lives?

Was she strong enough to lose everything a second time and still be standing in the end? Miriam wasn't sure.

Fredrick pushed his horse to go just a little faster. He was on his way into town to sort out this whole mess. When Miriam and Leah had arrived home from town he could see that something was wrong by the way Miriam avoided him more than usual and the confused broken look on Leah's face.

After Miriam had told him what had happened, he had found himself almost hopeful but then angry. Kitty was back? How could she disappear for more than two years and then just come waltzing back demanding Leah?

Soon he was at the steps of the hotel. After asking at the desk he found Kitty's room quickly and knocked hard.

When she answered the door, she took his breath away. She was a beauty as always.

"Fredrick, I'm so glad you came." She said sweetly.

"Let's get a coffee downstairs," he said, holding out his hand without any other comment.

Once they were seated Fredrick had gathered enough of his thoughts to formulate some questions.

"Why did you demand Leah from Miriam this afternoon?" He blurted out.

"She is my daughter." Kitty smugly shrugged her shoulders.

"You've been gone for more than two years." He accused angrily.

"Well, I wouldn't have made a scene, Fredrick, but you should have seen how that woman was treating her. It was despicable. I just wanted to make sure my baby was safe." Fredrick was surprised to see Kitty so honest and vulnerable.

"What do you mean how she was treating her? Miriam is wonderful with Leah."

"Around you maybe, but in the store, she pulled her hair and was talking so harshly to her- I just couldn't bear to watch."

As Kitty wiped tears from the corner of her eyes with her kerchief Fredrick felt a tug of doubt. Surely Miriam hadn't been treating Leah badly. Leah had been so excited about their activities the day before.

"I will talk to Miriam about this, but tell me, why did you come back?" He tried to still the battle that was raging on in his mind over his emotions.

"I missed you Fredrick. I realized that nothing was as important for me as you and Leah and I decided to come back. I just couldn't live without you anymore." Kitty leaned in, blinking her eyes sincerely and Fredrick almost felt as if she might kiss him.

"Kitty, I'm married again. We can't be together." He pulled back from the table. It was improper for him to even be here.

"Come Fredrick, isn't what we had something you want again? Don't you want me back again? After all, isn't that why you married her, to replace me?" Kitty's eyes were pleading, and Fredrick had to use all his strength to pull himself from the table.

"I have to go, Kitty. I'm sorry but it's too late." He shook his head sadly.

"It's never too late Fredrick. You can tell everyone it was just a mistake. I'll be waiting at the hotel in case you change your mind."

Fredrick made his way back home all the while trying to convince himself he wouldn't be changing his mind. Kitty had hurt him too much to let her back into his life, but then again there were moments where changing his mind felt like exactly like what he should do.

—-*—-

When Fredrick got home, he noticed that Leah had already been put to bed. Miriam sat on the sofa in front of the fire with a book open over her lap. A rush of warmth hit Fredrick that surprised him. Maybe he had just gotten used to seeing Miriam around.

She was staring at the book, but she wasn't reading it, she had the oddest look on her face. He had noticed the little worry lines at the corners of her eyes before. They were there again now. When she heard him she jumped a little.

"I didn't really expect you to be back so quickly." She said softly.

"Miriam, I know what you must think, but Kitty and I... Well it would be very hard for us to have feelings for one another again. In fact, it's mostly impossible. She left over two years ago, for the city and it's been rough on all of us. And, well, she is so shallow."

He paused and ran a hand through his hair. There. Now he had said it, the thing that had really bothered him about Kitty. She didn't seem to really care about him or about Leah. She seemed to care more for the city life than her family. He had let her physical beauty cloud his judgement.

"I feel like you haven't really given me a chance since I got here." Miriam looked up at him with sadness in her eyes. "I came here looking for a new family, but I'm not sure you were ready for one." She finished, her voice breaking.

"You're right. And I'm sorry. Today, seeing Kitty, well it made me realize how lucky I am to be given a second chance with you. Will you let me start over?" He asked, hoping she would say yes.

"I don't know, but I can try." Miriam stood from her seat and gave him a polite nod. "Goodnight Fredrick."

The way she said his name made him sad and the realization that he had been treating Miriam as if she were Kitty since she'd arrived hit him with a sudden force. Maybe he would be able to make it right.

—-*—-

Miriam paced back and forth. She had been pretty sure she couldn't ever come to love Fredrick, but his honesty and kindness from the night before had touched her heart. She suddenly saw everything he did in a new light. He was looking out for his heart and his family, something she knew a lot about.

After what had happened with her daughter and husband, she hadn't thought she would be married again, and she definitely never thought she'd have a family again. Now the thought of losing her fragile relationship with Leah and losing a second husband was tearing at every nerve. Determinedly she set her mind to her task at hand, she would save her new family, no matter what.

—-*—-

It had been more than four weeks since Kitty had made her reappearance in town. She hadn't wasted any time in re-establishing old connections and making town a miserable place for Miriam. Every time Miriam came to town, there was a new rumor circulating and more odd looks coming her way.

She had tried talking directly to Kitty about it but all she had received was a smug sneer and a warning that soon she'd be packing her bags to go back east. Miriam felt she couldn't bring it up with Fredrick because their friendship was just beginning to blossom and she wasn't sure he was ready to make a final choice. She noticed when he would stay up late at night staring at the family photo of him Kitty and Leah that he kept in his dresser drawer.

A firm knock on the door caused Miriam to shake herself from her thoughts. She was sure it must be Fredrick since he would be back any minute from dinner.

To her dismay, it was Kitty. She was as decked out as ever and this time sported a fancy picnic basket on her arm.

"I brought some lunch for my husband and daughter." She said in her syrupy voice.

"He's actually my husband now." Miriam corrected her forcefully. She had been the bigger person and turned herself away from all rumors and let her actions speak for themselves. But she couldn't allow this woman to insinuate that she wasn't married to Fredrick, that was just too much.

Fredrick appeared behind Kitty and took the porch steps two at a time.

"Kitty, what are you doing here?" His stern tone made Miriam's heart leap. Maybe he wasn't happy to see her either.

"I came calling to visit my daughter, and to bring her food. I know she doesn't eat enough. I don't believe your new wife knows how to care for a child properly." Kitty batted her lashes and gave a huge smile in Fredrick's direction. The way she touched his arm made Miriam sick. Did she not have any self-respect?

"Come in. I think Leah's just finishing with her homework." Fredrick extended his arm towards the door that Miriam was still blocking.

Soon they were settled in the living area and Kitty was embracing a still reluctant Leah and talking all about her experiences in the city. Miriam could tell her joyful memories of the past two years hurt Fredrick. His years had been anything but joyful, but it seemed that Kitty hadn't missed her daughter or husband for a minute and had only come back on a fling of boredom.

After Leah had finally gone off to bed Kitty still lingered and they sat awkwardly talking about little but the weather. Miriam fought a battle with sleep, but she wasn't about to retreat to her room and leave Kitty with her husband alone.

"Kitty, I need to be clear about something." Fredrick pulled both women's attention towards him.

"Of course, dear husband," she answered sweetly. Kitty placed her almost empty cup of coffee on the table beside her.

"If you decide to continue visiting, or staying in town for that matter of fact, it will only be with Leah." Fredrick took a long drink from his mug. "And I am no longer your husband so please stop addressing me as such."

"Oh, but it's for you too Fredrick, I only want to make the past right." She interrupted with an almost desperate tone to her voice.

"No, Kitty. It can't be. I am a married man now, and I am faithful to my wife." He looked towards Miriam with a look that made her feel warm.

"I need you to stop spreading lies about my wife, stop telling lies to our daughter and stop pursuing me. You lost that chance two years ago and you can't just come sweeping back into town and expect everyone to adjust to how it was before. If you continue I will have no choice but to deny you the privilege of visiting Leah as well."

Kitty stared back at him, her mouth hanging open in the most unladylike manner.

"I-I," she sputtered uncomfortably.

"I think it's time you go." Fredrick stood up and walked towards the door. Kitty followed with the most dumfounded expression as if she couldn't quite believe what was happening.

With one more withering look in Miriam's direction she took her leave.

After Fredrick closed the door firmly, he turned to Miriam.

"I – that was unexpected." Miriam said, meeting his eyes.

"She deserved it. I should have done that the minute that she walked back into our lives. I got caught up in the past from the minute you walked through that door. But these last few days, getting to know you with an open heart, has changed me, and my life."

Fredrick paused and drew a little closer.

"We may not know each other perfectly right now but one day we will, and hopefully we will be together for many years, Miriam. I know I don't deserve you but all I can do is ask for as many chances as I need."

"I don't deserve you either." Miriam said softly with a smile, and this time, her smile felt completely right.

—-*—-

Fredrick wasn't surprised a few days later, when he heard that Kitty had boarded the stagecoach the day before and gone back to the city where she had come from. She had finally taken the hint and decided to leave him to his new life. He sighed, relieved.

He climbed back into his saddle and turned the horse toward home with a satisfied smile on his face. Things were looking up. He was thankful that he had finally come to his senses. He clucked to his horse, urging him into a gallop. He couldn't wait to get home to his family!

Epilogue

Miriam bounced a chubby little boy on her hip. She didn't have much hips left now with the growing bump under her skirt.

"I'll take him mama." Leah's strong young hands reached up to take the gurgling baby from her and she gladly relinquished him.

Leah had been such a help with now almost two-year-old Freddy and Miriam was sure she would be equally as helpful with her second sibling who would be arriving soon.

"I'm home!" Fredrick's joyful voice called out as he came into the door.

"Pa!" Leah called out joyfully as she ran as best she could with the extra weight. Fredrick bent to give them a huge hug.

"I've missed you little ones." He laughed. "Did you help your Ma today?" He said, pretending to be stern.

Leah nodded with enthusiasm and Freddy mimicked her actions. Miriam laughed. Her family was complete and growing every day. She placed her hand on her belly as the awaiting member of the family gave a little kick.

"Hang in there, little guy. We'll be waiting for you when you're ready to come out," she chided softly, patting her stomach lovingly.

Fredrick pulled her into a hug.

"How was your day, sweet wife?" He smiled with a mischievous look in his eye.

"It was perfect, Fredrick, just perfect." And Miriam meant every word. She finally felt her life was perfect and despite their struggles, she wouldn't change one minute of it. It had made them all who they were.

ONE STARRY NIGHT

LAUREL BIRD

Chapter 1

Carlie watched the front door of her house slam shut. She couldn't help it. She hurried toward it and flung it open again. She saw the male figure walking quickly toward his truck. Carlie grit her teeth and refused to call him back once more.

But try as she might to control her body, she couldn't control the tears that started to stream down her cheeks. He got in his truck, slammed the door shut, and gave her an angry look before starting up his vehicle and squealing away.

"No!" Carlie said. She went in her house and curled up on her couch. This had not been the way it was supposed to go at all. Carlie had been suspected he had been cheating for the last two months, but she had tried to shove her suspicions away. They had been together for two years. She had thought there was no way he would actually cheat on her. She had never thought about cheating on him. Wasn't he just as loyal?

The problem was, what Carlie thought didn't change the facts. Her boyfriend had started yelling at her for snooping on his phone. He hadn't apologized for anything. He said he loved the other girl more anyway. It was just easier to keep Carlie than go through the whole break up. His words echoed through Carlie's head, and the sobs wracked her body again. She felt as if her whole world was falling apart.

"I can't believe this is happening!" Carlie cried in anguish. "I would never do anything like that to him. I thought- I thought he loved me." She shook her head. Her tears would begin to edge away, then a new memory of a comment he had made would flash through her head. "I can't do this," Carlie said pitifully. She wiped her tears away and collapsed on the couch.

Her tired eyes roamed over the living room restlessly. The first thing that caught her eye was a picture of the two of them at their one year anniversary. "No!" Carlie said, grabbed the picture frame and throwing it to the ground. Angry, Carlie threw her heel into it. Then, she turned and walked into the kitchen.

"I don't need him," Carlie said. She thought she had done all her crying when she had first begun suspecting that her boyfriend was cheating, but the sadness still washed over her in waves. "I should get out of here. I need to do something," Carlie said.

She grabbed a canteen and filled it with the hot chocolate she had been making for the two of them. She plopped in a few marshmallows and grabbed a blanket. There was a special spot at the end of the neighborhood. Carlie thought spending some time out under the stars might be good for her soul.

Doubling back into the kitchen, Carlie grabbed her coat from the back hook and put it on. It was promising to be a chilly night, even though it wasn't quite November. Carlie hiked down to the end of the neighborhood. The cold air felt fresh on her face, and she felt determined to enjoy the evening. She was free now. She didn't want to spend the rest of her life with a cheater anyway. It was better that she find out now then later down the line. That would be even more difficult.

Carlie tried to imagine a break up being even more difficult, but she couldn't. Carlie decided to push him out of her mind. She was going to look up at the stars, and. . .

Carlie tried to look up at the stars at that moment, but the street lights were too bright for her to see past them. "I'll see them soon enough," Carlie said to herself.

After about ten more minutes of walking, Carlie reached the end of the neighborhood. The street lights faded behind her as she stepped over the construction tape and climbed a mound to the grassy knoll. She always wanted to come out here and take time to enjoy the beautiful natural surroundings, but in her busy life, she never had time.

Carlie spread her blanket out on the hill and settled onto it, pulling the hot chocolate canteen close to her for warmth. She looked up at the stars and smiled. There were a lot out tonight. Carlie drank a few sips of the hot chocolate but found it was still too hot to drink. She lay down on the blanket and studied the sky. She tried to see if she could find any constellations, but she had never been very good with that sort of thing.

She smiled to herself as her eyes blinked sleepily shut. Suddenly, Carlie was wide awake. She was never sure if she fell asleep or just been drowsy, but she was awake now. Carlie swallowed slowly. What was she doing in the middle of a field? Oh yeah, now she remembered. But, why had she woken up?

Carlie slowly sat up and saw a man standing a few feet away. She opened her mouth and screamed.

Chapter 2

The shadow whipped around to her, and Carlie skittered back a crawl and a tumble. The man's shadow got smaller as he detached himself from another shape that she determined to be a telescope. Carlie studied him as the man came closer.

"Didn't mean to startle you," he said. "But I didn't think I was that ugly."

His attempt at a joke was ignored by Carlie as she sat up and studied him. "What- what are you doing here? Who are you?" When he got closer, Carlie could see that he was quite normal looking. He had glasses and was dressed in long pants and a long collared shirt.

"I'm Matthew," he said, extending his hand. Carlie shook it and invited him to sit on her blanket, never taking her eyes off him.

"Carlie," she said. "I don't you think you live in this neighborhood. I would have met you before, right?"

Matthew shrugged. "I'm from the next neighborhood over. I'm doing some research of the night skies."

Carlie smiled. This guy seemed like the kind of person who would have been called nerd in high school but then grew up to make something of himself. "What are you looking for?"

"Right now, I'm hoping to see Venus and Saturn when they cross orbits."

"Wait, what? Planets cross orbits?" Carlie laughed for the first time since her boyfriend had entered the house that night. "Sorry. I'm not very knowledgeable about that sort of thing. I thought those planets were pretty far apart."

"It's okay," Matthew said. "I'm an astronomer. I want to capture the moment, but I think it might be a few more hours."

"You're going to take a picture?"

"Yes, my telescope can take pictures. This is a fairly common occurrence compared to some others, but I've never been able to see it before. Sometimes, the night is too cloudy or the weather just isn't clear enough for me to catch a glimpse. It looks like tonight will be the night. Sorry," he paused. "I'm just babbling on to you about astronomy, and you're probably bored to death."

"No," Carlie quickly replied. "I don't mind at all. I think it's cool to learn about new things."

"What did you study, if you don't mind my asking, Carlie the mysterious woman who sleeps in the grass?"

Carlie laughed again. "I'm actually an English major."

"Really?" Matthew said. "What do you do?"

"I teach fourth grade. I love kids, so that's my kind of thing," Carlie said. "I thought I might do something a little more aspiring, like be a published author when I got out of school, but that doesn't pay a livable wage."

Matthew leaned back on his elbows. "What would you write about if you could write?"

"Well," Carlie paused. "I do write, actually. I just don't. . .publish it."

"Why not?" Matthew asked. Carlie felt odd that this stranger was so interested in her life, but he seemed nice enough. He wasn't trying to harass her; he was just trying to pass the hours until his special moment came.

Carlie shrugged, taking the time to evaluate why she wasn't pursuing what she loved. "It's a hard world to publish in. I'd have to pay an agent, and then companies could still reject my manuscripts. Besides, I don't know if they're really anything someone would want to read. They're more like things I write to help me process what's going on in my life."

"Like a journal," Matthew added.

"Sure, like a journal, except," Carlie's voice caught, and she muffled the sound with a sip from her hot chocolate. "Things always end happily."

Matthew looked at her. "Wouldn't that be great if life could always end just like we wanted it to?"

Carlie nodded. "In a book, no matter what hard times characters go through, they are still happy in the end."

"You know what's terrible," Matthew said, making Carlie look at him sharply. Matthew was the kind of guy who made you want to listen to what he was going to say. "In books, the story always ends just as characters are getting to that happy place in their lives. You see that as a good thing. I don't. I think it's better if they get to live out a bit of that happiness and not just have it in the end. It's like the eating the worst food you have ever eaten to be rewarded with a big chocolate cake in the end. But you only get to have half a bite."

Carlie laughed and lay back on the blanket. "Wow, you're going to make me think you're crazy. I never looked at it that way before."

"We're always in search of a happy ending, so busy looking for that happy ending, that we don't take the time right now to enjoy the happiness we already have."

"Where do all of these brilliant ideas come from?" Carlie asked.

Matthew laughed, and Carlie liked the sound of his laughter. It was deep and genuine. "My many, many years of experience."

Carlie looked around at him. "Oh, you're not so old. How old are you?"

"Twenty-nine," Matthew said. Carlie nodded. He was three years older than she was. Matthew pressed his watch, and it lit up. "I think it should happen in another hour."

Carlie smiled, but a little bit of her didn't want to end their conversation. She was having such a great time trading ideas with him.

"What brought you out here tonight?" Matthew asked. "You know what I'm doing, but I don't know what you're doing."

Carlie shrugged. "Sometimes, I just want to be close to nature and enjoy its beauty."

Matthew raised his eyebrows. "Alright. I'll assume you know how to do that while sleeping, then."

Carlie laughed and pushed his shoulder with her own. "Stop it! I didn't mean to sleep. That just happened. Besides, I had plenty of time to enjoy nature's beauty before I fell asleep."

Matthew smiled. "I'll be right back." He went over to his telescope and adjusted a few things, then he grabbed his bag and brought it over to the edge of the blanket. "Are you hungry?"

"That depends on what you have," Carlie said. "If it's something delicious, then I'm always ready for some of that."

Matthew smiled and took out a bag of chips and a container of fruit salad. "I don't know if this is what you would consider delicious, but it's junky and healthy at the same time, so that's what I chose to bring."

"Thanks," Carolyn said, taking the container's lid that Matthew had liberally sprinkled with fruit. "Here, I have hot chocolate if you want some."

They sat on the blanket sharing the food and hot chocolate, silent under the stars. Carlie glanced over at Matthew. The only light came from the stars, so she couldn't see him very well. What she did know was that no matter what he looked like, he was the kind of person that made you want to be around him.

"Oh!" Matthew jumped up after looking at his watch. "I need to go monitor my telescope!"

Chapter 3

Carlie watched as Matthew hurried away. He had a notebook, and he was furiously taking notes, though how he could see them was a mystery to Carlie. She watched him work and wondered what it would be like to know everything about the stars and to understand how the planets revolved.

"Carlie!" Matthew called, his voice seeming crude in the calm air. "Don't you want to come see?"

Of course, she did! Carlie jumped up, throwing a few pieces of fruit to the ground accidentally, and rushed over to Matthew's side.

"Okay, they're going to cross in about five minutes, so I'll need to be looking through at that point to take the pics. But I thought you might want to see them."

"Which planets? And what do they look like?"

"Saturn and Venus."

"They cross paths?" Carlie asked again, puzzled.

"Quick," Matthew said. He placed his hand on her arm and pulled her toward the telescope. "I'll explain to you afterward."

Carlie laughed and looked through the telescope, searching for something that she would call a planet.

"They're going to look like large stars, nothing more," Matthew instructed. "They should be centered in the telescope."

Carlie jumped back as though the telescope had stung her. "Hey! I saw them, but they're super close. You better get in there or you're going to miss them."

Matthew pressed his eye against the glass and began changing the telescope. Carlie heard a clicking noise, and she assumed he was taking pictures of the planets. She waited patiently until the deed was done. Matthew turned away from the telescope with a huge smile on his face.

"I got it," he said. "Did you see that?"

Carlie nodded, even though she had not understood exactly what she had seen. "That's awesome! I'm glad," Carlie said, nodding enthusiastically.

Matthew sighed then looked at Carlie. He seemed to realize that his goal was completed. Carlie wondered if he was going to pack up and leave. He had no other reason to stay.

"We should probably eat up that fruit," Matthew said. "It'll just go bad anyway if I take it home."

Carlie went back to the blanket and gathered the fruit that had fallen on the blanket. It was still good. She slowly forked each piece of fruit into her mouth. She wanted to ask Matthew more about his job, what he did, and his life, but the conversation felt awkward now.

"I guess you've got school tomorrow," Matthew finally said, as Carlie was finishing up her fruit.

"No," Carlie said. "It's Labor Day. That means vacation. You're not working tomorrow, or are you?"

Matthew gave her a startled look. "Well, science doesn't exactly work on the same schedule. I'll probably go into the office even though it's Labor Day. I might as well get some work done."

Carlie nodded. "So you're a workaholic then?"

Matthew grinned at her. "You write when you get home from school. Does that make you a workaholic?"

Carlie laughed. "Okay, you got me. We'll just settle it that we are both NOT workaholics. Deal?" She offered her hand to Matthew who took it, but he didn't shake it. Instead, he pulled her to her feet.

"Ready to go home?" he asked.

Carlie sighed and glanced down at the blanket that had offered her comfort for the last few hours. She decided that once Matthew had packed up, she would stay for a time more. Maybe she would sleep outside for the night. Carly smiled. "I think I'm going to stay a little longer."

"I was just thinking the same thing," Matthew said. "I'm not quite ready to go yet."

Carlie looked over at Matthew and made eye contact. His two pools of eyes, too dark to really make out were looking right back at her. Carlie's stomach rolled over.

"Do you want to explore?" Carlie asked. "I used to know these woods when I was a little girl. I can show you some pretty cool things."

"You lived here when you were a kid?" Matthew asked her.

Carlie shook her head. "Ironically, my best friend grew up in a house on this street. I came over here all the time. When I moved in here, it felt like I was moving into a familiar glove, not a new one that's all difficult to break in. Come on."

"I have a penlight if it'll help," Matthew said, leaving a cover on his telescope so that it would be protected from any possible rain. "I think we should be safe. The skies are clear."

Carlie smiled at him and pulled him away from the open meadow and into the trees. She released his hand once they were under the trees. The darkness had engulfed them.

"I assume you know where we're going, right?" Matthew said, teasing Carlie.

"No," she said. "Let's get lost." She grabbed his hand again, a total sense of abandon coming over her. She felt like a child again, throwing all of her worries to the wind as she picked her way along the barely visible path. "I don't think as many kids have been playing here now," Carlie said. "This path used to be wider and clearer."

"Probably has to do with the 'No Trespassing' sign in the front of this area."

Carlie shrugged. "Yeah, you're probably right. Good thing you and I are both daredevils." Carlie glanced down at their clasped hands, and a sick feeling cut through her. What was she trying to prove? She was flirting with a man she had just met, and. . .

Carlie looked up into Matthew's eyes again. She could see his white smile clearly shining in the dark. "You seem a little lost to me," Matthew said.

Carlie turned away from him, dropping his hand again. "No, I know exactly where I'm going, but I think you have a problem trusting me to guide you."

Matthew laughed. "Sure, think I'm strange because I have trouble trusting a woman I just met on a dark night."

Carlie joined his laughter. "You make me sound like a strange witch that appeared out of nowhere. Did you see me when you were setting up?"

"Well, even if I had been blind, I would have heard your snoring," Matthew said.

Carlie gave him a horrified look. "No! I wasn't snoring. Please tell me you are making that up." Matthew gave an impish shrug, and Carlie pushed his chest. "You big tease. I knew I didn't snore."

"I never said I was making it up," Matthew said. "Anyway, I wasn't going to wake you up, and there is no other place as good as that one for watching the planets."

Carlie nodded and led him forward. "Why don't you go first?" she suggested. "You have the light."

"Where is it that we're going?" Matthew asked.

Carlie smiled. That was her secret. He would find out soon enough.

"Be patient. Wait, and you will see."

"Alright," Matthew said, "But if I lead us the wrong way, it's not my fault."

Carlie stood aside and let him pass her on the small path. She got behind him and started following his tall figure as they worked their way over the childhood path.

"Looks like we've come to a fork," Matthew said. "Which way?"

"Right," Carlie said. They were almost there.

"Did you and your friend make this path?" Matthew asked.

Carlie nodded. "Yeah, we spent multiple days using a broom and picking out rocks, etc. Then, we walked on it so much, that it kind of became part of the forest."

"Sounds like a fun childhood," Matthew said. "I always wanted to be that sort of kid, but I was always the kid who stayed inside and played with Legos. Now, I stay inside all day and play with telescopes and star charts."

"Have you come to your happy ending?" Carlie asked, remembering their conversation from earlier.

Matthew raised his eyebrows. "I hope I haven't come to an ending, happy or not. I'm not ready for my life to be over yet."

"Guess you shouldn't have come into the woods with a strange woman then," Carlie said, laughing maniacally. Matthew turned to her and shone the light on his face to show his horror stricken expression.

"Hey, I have the light," he said. "I can leave you behind in the darkness to consider your evil behavior."

Carlie laughed again. "Oh, Matthew, you wouldn't dare. I can already tell you're too much of a gentleman."

Matthew turned and looked at her for a moment before he continued walking.

"There it is," Carlie said, pointing into the trees ahead. The ropes were a little older than she had remembered them. Even though she had moved into the neighborhood, she hadn't brought herself to visit their homemade ropes course and fort since she was fifteen or sixteen.

"Whoa!" Matthew said. "You made this?"

Carlie nodded. "My friend and her dad helped. I promise you; it's safe. At least, it was safe ten years ago."

Matthew went over and tugged on one of the ropes. It seemed to be holding on strong. "I know you say it's safe, and it feels nice and strong. But," Matthew shook his head. "I don't know I would risk my life on a dark night trying it out."

A little part of Carlie felt disappointed. She had wanted to return to her childhood. She had wanted to feel that free of worry again. But, she found that even without mounting the course, she still felt happier than she had in a long time.

"Paula and I used to do it all the time. We would time each other and see who was the fastest."

Matthew was examining the course piece by piece. "I think I missed out on this piece of my childhood," he said, smiling back at her. Carlie loved the way his teeth lit up in the dark.

"Look," Carlie said. "You can at least trust the swing, right?"

Matthew went over to the swing and pushed on it. It seemed trustworthy. "Let's sit," Matthew said, gesturing toward the bench.

Chapter 4

Carlie sat down on the bench next to Matthew and found herself automatically snuggling up to him, not that she usually snuggled up to strangers. It was just that he felt so comfortable, and familiar in an odd sort of way. Matthew put his arm around her, and Carlie smiled.

"I heard a quote, and I was just thinking about it," Carlie said, meditating deep things as Matthew clicked off the penlight and the sound of crickets began to fill the air. "It said, 'Was it really a bad day or was it just a bad five minutes that you milked all day?' Sometimes, I let bad things take over my life. It's hard not to blow them out of proportion."

Matthew's hand was slowly stroking Carlie's hair. It didn't feel strange at all. She felt as if she had known him for years. "I suffer the same. I think it's normal. You have to decide to be happy."

Carlie smiled and turned toward Matthew. "And right now, that decision isn't so hard. I'm deciding to be happy." She smiled at Matthew, and she could see him smiling back at her. "I guess I realized I don't need much to be happy."

"What do you need to be happy?" Matthew asked.

"Right now? All it took was a beautiful night, a blanket, and a strange man looking at the stars."

Matthew laughed. Carlie looked at him and felt an urge to kiss him. She wondered what his lips tasted like. Not hesitating at all, Carlie leaned forward, her eyes fluttering closed. She gently pressed her lips against his, and he leaned into her. Carlie felt the sparks fly as they kissed. She suddenly pulled back, her heart racing. Her breath was coming quickly as she looked at Matthew in a new light.

Carlie swallowed carefully and lay her head back on Matthew's chest, turning her mind back to the stars and the planets and other things.

"You're certainly not what I was expecting when I planned to go out stargazing tonight," Matthew said. Carlie's smile was sweet.

"You weren't what I was expecting either," Carlie replied. Carlie squinted as Matthew suddenly pulled out his phone and the bright light flared up. Matthew pressed a few buttons on his phone, and soft music began to play. It wasn't the sort of music Carlie had ever kept on her phone. It was the type of music that had lyrics that made you think, not lyrics that made you want to start dancing like crazy.

"You're a very deep man," Carlie said as she evaluated his music choice.

"Does that mean I'm hard to figure out?" Matthew asked.

Carlie shrugged. "I don't really know what to make of you. You're. . .I don't know. I feel like I could tell you anything."

"Tell me anything then," Matthew said. "I'm ready to listen."

Carlie sighed. "The truth is that I don't want reality to hit me."

"Are you running from something?"

"Pain, a lot of pain. I came out here to try to escape, even if I wasn't thinking that when I came. I didn't think I'd find someone to escape with."

"Where are we going?" Matthew asked. "If we're escaping, we should go somewhere good, where we wouldn't mind hiding for a while."

"Hawaii," Carlie said, the first tropical place that popped into her mind.

"Hawaii it is then," Matthew said, his hand resting across her shoulders and on her upper arm. "I love the beaches and the sound of the waves."

Carlie closed her eyes and imagined they were sitting on the edge of the beach, her toes ready to dig into the sand. "It would be warmer," she said. "We would dive into the cold water and feel refreshed."

"There would be seashells on the beach. I have a huge collection of shells. I still need a perfect conch, though."

"There's going to be the perfect conch shell there," Carlie said. "Warm sand, and cold water. A beautiful sunset with an array of colors. Oh, I wish I could be there right now." Carlie opened her eyes to the chilly weather and the dark night and felt disappointed. She felt as though her night had been a little spoiled.

"Come on," Matthew said, standing and fully bringing Carlie out of her imagination. "Let's go."

"Where to?" Carlie crinkled her nose.

"I too may have my share of secrets," Matthew announced.

Carlie laughed. "What do you know about these woods?"

"I didn't say it had to do with these woods," Matthew said, taking Carlie's hand. He led her through the dark, following the path. Carlie held his hand tightly. She told herself it was for warmth, but in reality,

Matthew was tugging at more than just her hand. He had a grip on her attention, and Carlie didn't seem able to pull it away.

Out under the stars once again, Matthew turned to Carlie and took both of her hands. Carlie laughed aloud. She hadn't felt this happy and free since she was a child. Carlie broke away from one of Matthew's hands and pulled him up the hill at a running pace. Closing her eyes, Carlie pulled Matthew close and began swaying to the music he still had playing softly from his pocket.

Matthew laughed his low laugh and squeezed her tightly. They swayed back and forth to the music, then Matthew tried to spin Carlie away from him. It didn't work as well as he had been planning it, and Carlie tumbled to the ground. She laughed as she looked up at Matthew who was looking quite embarrassed.

"I guess you can tell I haven't had much practice dancing. Brooms turn a lot easier you know."

Carlie laughed and reached up for the hand Matthew was offering her. "I guess I'll have to help you get some practice in," Carlie said.

Matthew held her close. "I'd like that," he whispered. Carlie cuddled up to him as they danced, slowly moving back and forth. The music and the swaying movement made Carlie realize how tired she was. She didn't want the night to end, though, and she forced herself to stay awake.

"Are you ready to practice that spin again?" Matthew asked.

Carlie nodded and followed Matthew's lead. He dipped her, and Carlie saw the world upside down for a few moments before he brought her back up. She smiled at him. "You're a good dancer," she said, just as the song ended.

"That is definitely a first," Matthew said. "I've never heard those words before, at least not directed at me."

"They should have been," Carlie said.

Matthew raised his eyebrows. "Because I'm excellent at throwing girls on the floor?"

His question hung in the air, and they both started laughing.

"Well," Carlie said. "You've already brushed up on that skill, and your others are all excellent."

Matthew hugged Carlie tightly. "Thanks. That's really sweet of you."

"I think my legs are getting tired," Carlie said. "Do you need to go back?" What she really wanted to do was plead him to stay with her just a little longer. She wasn't ready for their night to end. She wanted to spend just a little more time with this man who had challenged her generic perspective on life.

Chapter 5

"I can stay a little bit longer, but then I should really get to sleep. You too," Matthew said as they walked over to the blanket. Carlie collapsed onto it. It didn't feel nearly as warm as she had remembered it. She knew their time was ticking away, and she wanted to just stop the clock. She didn't know what time it was, and she didn't want to know either. She avoided looking at Matthew's watch when he lit it up. "It's-"

"Stop! I don't want to know," Carlie said as Matthew sat then lay next to her. "I don't want to crash into reality yet. I just want to remain in our little paradise a little longer."

Matthew put his arm around her and pulled her close. Carlie curled her legs up and leaned against him. "Why are you so scared of going back into reality?"

Matthew's words were searching for truth, and Carlie was too scared to give it to him. "I- I have a lot going on right now. I don't want to enter reality and feel the same emotions I was feeling earlier. It's better here." Carlie had split the two in her mind, and she didn't want the magical night to end.

Matthew kissed Carlie's hair gently, and it made her smile up at the stars.

"I'm sorry," he said.

Carlie closed her eyes. "it's not your fault. Life is like that, huh? It throws you curveballs just to make sure you still know how to jump."

"Good thing you can still jump," Matthew said, kissing her hair again.

"I think I'm crippled," Carlie said, the tears coming to her eyes as the pain of the encounter, which now seemed days ago, hit her again. Matthew saw up and looked at her. He saw the tears and gently wiped the away.

"Nothing can cripple you forever unless you let it. Do you understand? You are in charge of your life."

Carlie knew his words were meant to be encouraging, but she just felt too sad to be encouraged back to a smile. She sat up and folded herself into Matthew's arms. Her tears came. They weren't ugly sobs that racked her whole body but silent streams that blinded her. When she seemed to have nothing left, she sat back. "You're a brave one," she said to Matthew. "You're not scared off by anything."

"I generally like to think I'm not a scaredy-cat."

Carlie burst into a smile that caused a snot bubble to blow out of her nose. Carlie was embarrassed as she wiped it away. She turned her face away, but Matthew was smiling down on her, not the kind of mean smile but a gentle, teasing smile.

"I'm still not scared," Matthew said.

"You should probably take the warnings and run far away," Carlie warned. But even she did not take her own advice. She leaned against Matthew again. The stars seemed different. Did they change during the night? She started to ask Matthew, but she knew he might go down a long astronomical explanation that would confuse more than help her. She just sat, letting her thoughts wash over her.

Her eyes started closing, and she felt as though she could go to sleep right there. Matthew suddenly moved, causing her to startle and sit up. "I have one thing I want to show you," Matthew said. He pulled his bag a few inches closer and rustled around. Carlie sat up and tried to orient herself.

Matthew pulled out a stone from his bag. He admired the stone for a minute then passed it on to Carlie. Carlie looked at it. "What is it?" she asked. That answer was obvious. Her real question was why was he showing her this thing.

"It's a stone from a meteorite," Matthew said.

Carlie's eyebrows rose. "A real meteorite?"

"No," Matthew said. "The fake one that landed a few towns over and made a massive hole."

"When did that happen?" Carlie handled the stone, fingering its curves and edges.

"It was before we were both born, but it's still there off the edge of town."

"I don't know how I never heard of that," Carlie said.

"This stone reminds me that we're so small. The world, the planets, the solar systems, are enormous. Our little lives are nothing in comparison. It helps remind me that my problems will pass. Why don't you keep it?"

Carlie nodded. "Thank you." She pocketed the stone. It felt warm in her pocket.

"We should probably go," Matthew said, standing and pulling her to her feet.

Carlie rubbed her eyes and stood stupidly for a few minutes as she tried to wake up. When she was able to function, she gathered her blanket and handed Matthew his things to put in his bag. Once she had her canteen, Carlie was ready to go. She watched Matthew pack up his telescope and stow it carefully in the back of his car. Finally, Matthew shut the door, and Carlie knew what came now.

"I can drive you to your house," Matthew said. "Where do you live?"

Carlie smiled, but she shook her head. "Thanks, but I'd like to walk. It's not far. I live just up this street."

Matthew nodded. He took a step forward then paused. "Maybe, I don't know. I'd. . .like your number. Can I?" Carlie slowly nodded. He pulled out his phone and typed the number in. He tucked his phone away, and they both looked at each other awkwardly.

Finally, Matthew took a step forward, and Carlie turned her lips up toward him. He kissed her gently, just as softly as a whisper of wind. As he stepped back, Carlie wanted to pull him toward her again, but she didn't. She watched him get in his car and start it up. The two red taillights faded into the distance, and Carlie was alone again.

She began the walk back to her house, back to reality, the warmth of Matthew's hand and kiss still lingering on her. Carlie wondered if in the morning light, her magical night would have disappeared. Would Matthew be the same person she had met on the grassy knoll? Was she even the same person she had been tonight?

Carlie hadn't felt the need to hide herself from Matthew. He was completely real. Carlie climbed into her bed, spreading the blanket from the meadow on her, not caring about the bits of grass. Sometimes, fantasy is better than reality.

The scent of Matthew's cologne lingered on the blanket, and as Carlie fell into her dreams, she knew that Mathew was the kind of man worth being real for.

AMISH SUNSET

NANCY MANN

Chapter I

Rain decorated the grassy fields of Lancaster County. The sky was a cloud grey, the sun remaining absent as the county mourned for the loss of William Bradshire, a carpenter that had been known throughout the county for his kindness and love towards the people around him.

Friends and family had gathered in the county's cemetery for William's funeral, one of the mourners being William's love, Mary Lee Warner. Out of everyone there, Mary was the most damaged from it. William's parents had passed on early in his life due to illnesses and the remaining family he had weren't as close. If anything, Mary was the only one there who truly was family to him.

As Bishop David spoke about his memories with William, Mary thought to herself how God could do such a thing, to take away an innocent being this early in his life. William was only in his mid-twenties, like Mary. He had so much to experience in his life, but it was stripped away from him so early due to the accident.

"If anyone has anything to say, speak now." Bishop David said, stepping back and letting anyone step forward to speak.

There was a long pause, silence being present as Mary thought to herself. Eventually, she took a step forward, standing in front of the casket as she let out a depressed sigh.

"William...had a beautiful soul," Mary said quietly, holding onto a wildflower, "a soul that I have yet to find in any other human being."

Everyone was watching her speak, seeing what Mary had in her hand and what she had to say about William being gone.

"I can't imagine not meeting him in my life...all the memories we've made together...all the laughter, the love...I'm going to miss it." Mary spoke as tears ran down her cheeks. "I don't know if I will find another William in my life."

Some of William's family members began to have tears fall too as they listened to Mary's words about their lost kin. Mary soon stepped back from the casket, having finished speaking on the behalf of William's death. Bishop David soon stepped forward again, wiping some tears from his own eyes.

"Thank you Mary...I will say, before I close in prayer, that it will be difficult to find another William in our lives." Bishop David said to Mary before opening his Bible.

Verses from the Bible were soon spoken out loud, everybody bowing their heads in prayer as Bishop David spoke. While everyone listened, Mary wasn't listening to the verses, in fact, she was in her own mind at this point.

"Why God...why would you take William away from me?" Mary thought to herself. "William didn't even get half way into his life...why would you take him now?"

As she struggled with the idea of William passing on, Bishop David finished reading the verses, quietly speaking the word amen as he closed his Bible, everybody soon leaving the scene of the funeral, letting the casket to be lowered into the grave. While the casket lowered, Mary was the only one present, witnessing her love's final presence on the surface of Earth.

In regards to funeral traditions of the Amish, flowers were not placed on the casket. For Mary though, traditions meant nothing to her in this occasion. She took the wildflower that she was holding in her hand and tossed it down into the undug grave, letting it land on the coffin before the gravediggers began to bury the coffin.

"I love you so much William." Mary said as the coffin soon disappeared from the soil piling on top. Tears continued to fall onto the soil as she left the site of the funeral.

Chapter II

Several years later...the county had returned back to its normal ways, except for Mary. Ever since William passed away, Mary wasn't her old self. Her old cheerful personality had passed on as well, leaving her a closed up, emotionless woman in her mid-twenties.

She tried to return back to a normal life by going to church, seeing if God might be able to help her find peace, but the more she went the church, the more she began to question God. At times, she would find herself being angry at God for taking William away this early in his life. Eventually, Mary stopped going to church, which brought the concern of Bishop David, leading him to go to Mary's home.

Her house was a little way from town, being near one of the farms. She lived in a large house that belonged to William and his parents. Now that William passed on, Mary now owned the house and lived in it by herself.

Bishop David knocked on the front door, waiting for it to be opened. It took a few knocks before the door finally opened, Mary standing there in a stone grey dress.

"Yes?" Mary quietly said, looking at him with her expressionless face.

"May I come in?" Bishop David asked softly, his expression being hopeful that she would accept his request.

Mary let out a quiet sigh before she nodded, stepping out of the way for Bishop David to come in.

"Thank you...Mary." He said, soon walking into her home, looking around.

Mary shut the door behind Bishop David, walking past him and sitting down on a chair in the living room, continuing what she was doing before he knocked. When Bishop David sat down across from her, he noticed that she was knitting a quilt.

"Oh…I see that you've been busy with making a quilt." Bishop David said, giving Mary a gentle smile.

"Quilts. I've been busy making quilts." She said quickly, pointing in the corner to a basket of several quilts.

Bishop David was surprised by the amount of quilts she had made. "That's quite the number of quilts Mary." He said with a small laugh after.

Mary raised her eyebrows as she continued to knit the quilt. "I've found that work is one of the few things that keeps me from thinking about the past." She said softly, not making eye contact with Bishop David.

"Oh…well…if that's what helps you find peace." He said quietly, rubbing the back of his neck before he finally decided to talk about why he wanted to talk to her. "Mary…I'm worried about you."

She heard Bishop David, stopping for a second before she continued knitting the quilt. "Why?" Mary questioned him.

"I'm concerned for you because you haven't been going to church for months." Bishop David finally said, looking at her with a worried expression. "You were always an avid church-goer when William…" He said before realizing what he said, stopping in mid-sentence.

Mary immediately looked up when Bishop David brought up William, her knitting ceasing before she let out a sigh of disbelief escape her lips. She set the quilt and knitting needle down. "Please, do not ever bring up William to me again when comparing me to then and now." Mary said, her voice trembling as she had grown an upset expression.

Bishop David had become silent as he listened to Mary finally speak to him.

"I'm no longer the Mary from then because of the events that happened, and if you want to visit me and tell me how I use to love church and that you're concerned with me not being there on Sundays, then don't even speak, you're wasting your breath." Mary said to him, her eyes staring into his intensely.

Bishop David heard everything she was saying before he let out a sigh of sympathy. "I'm sorry Mary that you're like this...I didn't come here today to chastise you about not attending church. I came here because I'm really concerned for what you've become. I want happiness for you, I want you to have that cheerful personality that everybody knew you for." He said softly, standing up from sitting, looking down at her. "Always remember Mary, we all face events in life that we don't want, but it's all a part of God's plan for something greater."

Mary just glared at him the whole time he spoke, not even acknowledging the things he said. "I would like you to leave."

Bishop David heard her request and nodded softly, walking away from where they were at and leaving the house.

She had watched him leave through the windows before she finally reached for her knitting needles and quilt, continuing to knit as she thought about what he said about God having a plan for everyone. To her, God's plan was killing William and taking away something that she loved most in the world, when she didn't have anyone else.

"Forget God." Mary said to herself quietly, having completely lost faith and love in God.

Chapter III

One stormy night soon had arrived in Lancaster County. Rain had arrived over the town and fields, the sound of sharp pellets hitting the roofs and windows of each building. The window whirled between each building, the sounds of wind wailing could be heard by anyone who was awake.

While the storm stayed present in the county, Mary was asleep in her bed, although she wasn't sleeping soundly. The red-headed woman was having a nightmare, causing her to toss back and forth in her sleep before some sort of sound interrupted her slumber.

KNOCK KNOCK KNOCK

Mary sat right up from her bed like a vampire in a coffin, rubbing her eyes. "What on Earth?" She said to herself, looking around the room as she wondered what caused her to wake up.

KNOCK KNOCK KNOCK

This time, the red-head heard the solution to the noise. "Who could be at my door in the middle of the night?" Mary got out of her bed, wrapping her blanket around herself to cover her nightgown. She made her way down the stairs of her home before seeing the front door. Once she got to the door, she slowly opened it, seeing who it was.

There was a man, about her age, with a young daughter about six-years-old. They were wet from head to toe, shivering as they looked at Mary.

"Please...do you have room in your home for my child and I? We come from far away to Lancaster County...we have no home, no food." The man said, his tone being a desperate one.

Mary had no idea that this was what waited for her on the other side of the door. "I...Well..." She looked at the two before she finally nodded quickly, stepping out of the way.

"Oh thank you...thank you!" The man said happily and emotionally. He quickly moved inside, Mary shutting the door behind the two. Even though they were inside, away from the rain, they still were shivering in the dark home. Mary saw how cold they were and immediately knew what they needed.

She quickly went over to the fireplace in the living room, taking two logs that were on the side of the hearth in a pile and putting them inside the fireplace. After a few attempts of trying to get a fire started, she eventually managed to do so, an orange glow illuminating the living room.

Once the man saw the fire, he moved his daughter close to the fireplace, trying to get her as warm as possible. Mary saw what he was trying to do and quickly went over to the eight-year-old, wrapping her blanket around the child. The man soon began to dry off her daughter while at the same time trying to get her warm.

"There you go...nice and warm now. Away from the cold rain." He said quietly to his daughter, holding her close as he sat in front of the fireplace with her.

The daughter shivered still, but the warmth from the fire and the blanket caused the shivering to decrease as the time went by.

Mary stood behind the two, watching them and making sure that they were okay. "Are you warm enough?" She asked them, having held one of the quilts she had made in her hands to give to the man.

"Yes...thank you kind miss." He said quietly, holding his daughter close before taking the quilt from Mary, wrapping it around himself.

With the two warming themselves up from the fire, Mary decided to grab another quilt for herself before sitting down on her couch. She wrapped the quilt around her body so she could be warm too. Since she now had two "guests" in her home, she didn't want to go upstairs, back to bed, with the knowledge that two strangers were downstairs in her home, two people who she had no idea who they were.

"Maybe they're thieves," Mary thought to herself, studying the two strangers. "Although...she looks pretty young to be a thief." She finally decided to speak up, wanting to figure out who they were. "Where did you two come from?"

The man looked back at her, hearing her question before he began to reply to her. "We came from Somerset County." The man answered, still trying to warm up his daughter.

"Oh...that's far from here." Mary replied, sitting down on her couch, looking at the man.

"It very much is..." The man nodded, looking at her. "Do you know if there's any housing here in Lancaster County?"

Mary heard her question before she shrugged. "I'm not too sure. Are you looking for a place to stay?"

The man nodded, looking down at his daughter. She had fallen into slumber and had a warm expression on her face and had stopped shivering, indicating she was no longer freezing. "Yes."

She heard him and asked some more questions in order to get to know him. "Why Lancaster County? I'm sure there's plenty of other settlements along the way."

"I just," The man began to say, rubbing the back of his neck nervously, "I don't know...I guess I've heard a lot of great things about Lancaster. Figured that it would be a great place for my daughter to grow up in."

Mary nodded when he stated that it'd be a good place for his daughter to grow up in. "Lancaster really is a nice place to grow up in...a good place to start a fam-" she began to say before stopping when she was about to say "family." It reminded her of what she has always wanted to have and that made her think of William and her. "Well, it's a good place to meet nice and caring people."

The man saw her reaction when she was talking about family, but decided not to question it in order to remain polite. "That's good to hear...by the way," the man began to say, looking at her once again, "what is your name?"

She heard him and replied softly. "Mary...my name is Mary Lee Warner."

When the man heard her, he smiled softly. "That's a beautiful name."

Mary smiled softly when he complimented her name. "What about you? What's your name?"

"Robert." He said quietly, before looking down at his daughter, gently stroking her hair. "The little one is Miriam."

Chapter IV

The next morning had arrived, the rain was now gone, the only trace of rain being the puddles in the dirt. Mary decided to help Robert and Miriam out by going down to the church to see Bishop David could help them out.

Entering the church, there were only a few people present in the pews, praying to the Lord about whatever comes to their attention. Bishop David was not preaching, considering it was a Tuesday, so chances were he was at his home.

"Doesn't look like he's here." Mary said, turning around and leading Robert and Miriam out.

"Who are we looking for exactly?" Robert said, holding his daughter's hand as they walked towards Bishop David's house.

"We're looking for David, Lancaster County's bishop. He might be able to help you out with moving here." Mary replied, reaching the bishop's house before knocking on the door. Not too long after the knock, the door opened, Bishop David standing there.

"Mary?" He said, a little surprised. "What brings you here today?"

Mary explained the whole story to him, telling the bishop that Robert and Miriam showed up in the middle of the night, needing a place to stay and that they wanted to move to Lancaster.

"I see..." Bishop David said quietly, scratching his beard as he thought about it. "Unfortunately, there isn't any houses available right now."

Mary heard the news and let out a quiet groan. "So where will they stay if they don't have a home?"

Bishop David heard her before looking at the two, looking at Mary again. "Can I talk to you privately Mary?"

Mary was confused as to why, but nodded as she stepped inside the bishop's house. "What did you want to talk to me about?"

Bishop David looked at her before he let out a quiet sigh. "I wanted to talk to you privately about where they're going to stay. I believe they should continue living at your house until a new house can be built here in the county."

She listened to what he said before hearing his statement about the two staying at her home. "What? No. I can't have people living at my house."

Bishop David gave her a confused look. "Why not? You have one of the biggest houses here in Lancaster County. You're not living with anyone. There's plenty of room in the house for someone."

"Because, I don't have enough food to feed two more people. I don't want to start housing people." Mary was quick to say, folding her arms. "I can't let strangers come into my home and make themselves acquainted to the hou-"

"Mary." Bishop David interrupted, clearly showing he was getting irritated with her. "Enough with the excuses. I'm not going to force you to let them in. I'm only suggesting you give the two of them a home. It's not permanent, but where else are they going to go?" He asked Mary, looking at her with a serious expression. "They can't move into anyone else's home. They all have families, rather large ones too."

She listened to him, looking into his eyes as she thought about everything he was saying. Bishop David was right in many ways. Most families in the county had large families, homes that were already crowded. With Mary's house, it was just her. He even said that it wasn't permanent, so it'd be something that Mary didn't have to deal with for too long.

"I guess...I could have them stay for a little while." Mary finally admitted, realizing that she could be a little generous.

"Thank you Mary." Bishop David said before leading her back outside, now facing Robert. "We will discuss adding a house whenever I meet my colleagues. Until we can get a house added to the county, you'll have to stay with Mary for the time being."

Robert listened to what Bishop David said, nodding softly. "Okay, thank you."

Bishop David smiled softly, heading back into the house before closing the door.

Robert and Miriam turned toward Mary, looking at her. "So...are we going to back to the nice lady's house?" Miriam asked her father.

Mary heard her and couldn't help but smile. "Yes...yes you are."

Robert watched the two interact before he couldn't help but smile, seeing this stranger being so nice to his daughter.

"Alright. Let's head back to the house so I can get a room prepped up for you two." Mary said, clapping her hands together when she knew what she needed to do.

Chapter V

A couple of months passed by in Mary's household. The two strangers that had showed up on her doorstep were now friends of hers, having brightened up the household little by little. As Mary got to know Robert, he started feeling more and more comfortable around him, the two even joking around with each other.

With Miriam, she started to look up towards Mary as a mother figure, every now and then the little girl called Mary mom. Mary would hear this and laugh, finding it humorous that Robert's daughter called her mom.

While everyone was getting along just fine, Mary started to remember William again, every time she looked at Robert. There was something about Robert that reminded her of William. It might've been the way he made her laugh or the way he showed kindness to people. Whatever it was, Mary could see William through Robert, which made her think about if she found another William in her life.

It was now 6 PM and Robert and Miriam had finished eating dinner with Mary. When they finished, Robert decided to take Miriam to bed, since she started dozing off during dinner. Once she was in bed, she was out cold.

"She must've been really tired today. Miriam never goes to bed this early." Robert said, walking back into the kitchen. "I don't blame her...she didn't sleep that well last night."

"Oh poor thing." Mary said, cleaning the dishes in the sink. "I hope she rests well tonight."

"She probably will." Robert said, walking over before leaning against the counter. "So...what do you want to do?"

Mary continued to wash the dishes before she stopped, soon looking at him. "What do you mean?"

"Well I mean...Miriam is in bed early. Do you want to go out for a walk?" Robert replied, looking at her and waiting to hear an answer.

She looked at him before looking down at the dishes, thinking about his offer before setting the plates down. "I would enjoy that."

He smiled brightly before he walked out of the kitchen, planning on getting his jacket.

———

It didn't take long before the two were on an adventure, walking around the county in the early evening. The sky was an vibrant orange, the sun easing itself behind the hills.

"Wow...that's a beautiful sunset." Robert said softly, looking at it.

"It sure is." Mary said quietly, looking at it before she looked at Robert. With the two of them having grown closer, she soon started to think more in regards of making their relationship a bit more than friends. "Can I show you something?"

Robert heard her, turning his head and looking at her before he smiled softly. "Yeah of course."

Mary smiled brightly before leading him into the woods, walking in a certain direction. As for Robert, he wasn't sure where she was taking him, which made him a little nervous. Eventually, the two arrived in a rather large open area in the woods, a grass area that was decorated with wildflowers.

"Wow..." Robert quietly said to himself, stepping forward and starting to walk towards the flowers. "They're beautiful."

Mary stood behind Robert, watching his response before walking with him again. "I know. I love coming to this place. It reminds me of so many happy memories." She said before she began to lay down in the grass, looking at the sky that had become as orange as a Doris Longwing Butterfly's wing.

Robert watched what she did before he followed her actions, lying next to her as the two watched the sky. "You have quite the spot...especially one that you value." He smiled softly, relaxing on the grass.

The two watched the sky for a few, enjoying the time to relax with each other. Eventually, Robert spoke up, a question that had been resonating within him.

"How come you didn't want to let us live with you a few months ago?" He quietly said, still looking at the sky, some clouds gently moving along in the sky.

Mary heard him and gave him a confused look. "What do you mean?"

"You were talking to Bishop David the morning after the rainstorm. You told him that you didn't want anyone staying at the house because you didn't have enough food and didn't want housing people. Part of me though doesn't believe that."

Mary listened to what Robert was saying, her expression staying confused before her expression became more of a look of hesitant.

"There's something more than not enough food and not wanting to house people huh? You don't have to tell me, but just know I'm here if you want to talk." Robert said quietly, wanting to assure that she could trust him.

She listened to what he said before she began biting her own lip, thinking to herself before she let out a quiet sigh. "There is...there's a lot more to it. I think it's fair that you should know."

He heard her response to his question and turned onto his side, looking at her now as she began to speak about what the reason for not wanting anyone to live with her.

"It all has to do with a man I loved...a man named William." Mary said quietly.

Chapter VI

William Bradshire...a carpenter of Lancaster County. Most of the county knew him as the kind man who cared about everyone around him, even the ones who didn't care for him. William was the prime example of what it means to follow Christ's footsteps. He showed a strong love towards God, helped out around his community, showed love towards everyone, taught the youth about the Bible, and that's just the peak of the iceberg.

Sometimes in life though, bad things can occur that change one's life. For William, it was losing his parents at the age of eighteen. With his parents gone, he now owned the house, but that meant nothing to William. For a long time, he had struggled with the fact that his parents were gone, but during this time, he still continued to help people, having put them first before himself.

A great example of William putting others first was one cold, dark night. There was a knock on his door, the knock having echoed the entire silent household. When William opened his front door, he found a shivering girl his age, looking up at him. This girl was Mary.

The young girl had ran away from home, angry at her parents and her peers around her community. She was looking for a place to stay, which was she ended up on William's doorstep, a stranger to him. William was caring enough to immediately let her in; he even allowed her to stay as long as she needed. Even though she could've left any time, she found herself a priceless friendship.

Eventually, as time progressed, the redhead soon fell in love with William, the same happening with the boy. The two ended up revealing their love for each other when they discovered and rested in the grass area in the woods with the wildflowers. Ever since then, they were two peas in a pod.

As time progressed, they became closer and closer, almost being one soul. Mary began helping out in the community with him while developing a strong love of God since William introduced her to Him. Eventually, William decided that he was going to ask Mary for her hand in marriage, but his colleagues asked for his help in finishing the construction of a barn.

Unfortunately, William never had the chance to pop the question due to the accident. While he was watching his colleagues raise one of the barn walls up by pulling it up with ropes, the ropes snapped and the wall soon fell on William, his chances of escaping the wall very low with how fast the whole situation took. Sadly, William didn't survive the heavy barn wall crushing him.

Word soon got out around the county about William dying from the accident, which Mary soon heard about. She was devastated, crushed, her heart torn into pieces for the loss of her one true love.

After William had passed, Mary was given the house, considering she basically lived there and was a member of the community. During this time, Mary closed herself off from the rest of the world, locking herself away in her home, mourning the loss of William. She even decided to not let anyone into the house after the loss in order to keep the house peaceful, like it was when William and her were in it.

Even in the present, Mary still has nightmares about the whole incident, nightmares that remind her of the loss of William.

"If only I were there to stop him...to get him out of the way...If only I were there...he'd still be alive."

Chapter VII

Once Mary finished telling Robert the story, she had developed some tears from the memory of William's death.

"Now you know why I don't let anyone into the house...I know...it sounds insane, for the girlfriend of someone who has departed to keep the house like a temple. You must think I'm crazy..." Mary said quietly, wiping her tears.

"Oh no..." Robert said, looking at her. "I don't think you're insane at all...I can see why you value the house so much. All the memories with William...the laughter...the peace...everything about it...you don't want anyone to ruin this place for you." He said softly, gently resting his hand on hers. "I'm sorry...I didn't know this was the reason why you didn't want us here."

Mary heard him and finally broke down, tears rolling down her cheeks as she covered her face with her hands, muffled crying heard behind it. Robert reached for her and wrapped his arms around her, holding her close as he embraced her.

"Shhh...it's okay...Mary." Robert quietly said, stroking her hair gently to calm her down. "It's okay..."

After years of suppressing the memories of William and her, the pain she has endured from remembering his death, the many tears she had held back, she finally broke down and let her tears flow.

"I miss him so much...every day I wish I could see him again...tell him that I wish I could've saved him from the wall...I wish I could've done something." She said, pressing her face against Robert's shoulder as she shook from her crying.

"You couldn't do anything Mary...you had no idea that would happen..." Robert said softly, continuing to hold her close as she cried against him. "Look on the bright side...with William having a strong love for God, he's finally in Heaven where he can be with God...walk along with him...talk to him...laugh with him."

With Robert's words entering Mary's ears, it made her cry more. He was right in the sense that she wouldn't have known and that he's in a better place now. Her heart ached as she recalled all the memories of William from when they met to his death. All the memories were mainly happy and ones that would make her laugh whenever she looked back to them. Even though William was gone, she remembered one thing...William lives on through her. The memories, the house, the ideology, everything that William was made up of lives on through Mary. With this thought, she felt like she could finally get over the tragedy of losing William and achieve peace.

"Thank you...Robert...Thank you." Mary said quietly, looking up at him with tears in her eyes.

Robert looked down at her, confused as to why she was telling him thank you. "For what?" He laughed gently, wiping the tears away from her eyes.

"For saying all of those things about William and I...I've spent all these years holding onto William's tragedy and blaming myself for not being able to help him, but now I can finally find peace and let go of the tragedy...thank you...Robert." She finally said, looking at him as she gently reached up, stroking his cheek before she finally decided to lean in, kissing him gently.

Robert was caught off guard with the kiss, his eyebrows raising as she held her in his arms. Eventually, she broke the kiss, resting her head on his should. "Let's go back home...it's getting late." Mary said quietly, her eyes now closed.

Even though Robert had thought about pushing their relationship to another level, there was something that was holding him from reaching that level, something that had followed him from his previous home.

Chapter VIII

Many weeks had passed by since Mary told Robert about her past. Mary was in a much brighter mood, slowly building herself up again by socializing with people, going to church again, which made Bishop David happy, and she started wearing colorful clothes again.

Robert was thinking about what Mary had done in the wildflower area in the woods on the porch. He wanted to moved towards the next step, but the past was catching up with him.

"Hey!" Mary called out, coming up to the house with Miriam. "We've got dinner!"

He snapped back into reality, smiling gently when he saw the two. "Oh...that's wonderful. Looks delicious." Robert said, standing up and helping them take the food inside the house.

"I decided to cook something special for you...to thank you for helping me return back to my old self again."

Robert smiled and chuckled nervously, rubbing the back of his neck. "Oh...you don't have to do that."

"But papa," Miriam spoke out, looking at him, "look at the food! It looks delicious! At least let mom...Mary cook it for me."

Both Robert and Mary laughed at Miriam's comment, Mary picking her up and holding her.

"Okay, well if Robert doesn't want his special dinner, then I'll cook it for you." She said, walking in with the child.

"That'd be fantastic!" Miriam exclaimed happily.

Robert followed behind the two with the groceries, his expression being lost in thought as he thought about the past.

Dinner time soon arrived, everyone now seated at the table as they waited for Mary to come in with the special dinner.

"Whatever she's cooking, it smells delicious." Miriam said, excited to eat.

In a matter of minutes, Mary came out with a cooked turkey, the skin being a golden crisp.

Even though Robert wasn't asking for a special dinner, he was impressed with how the turkey came out. "Wow, looks really good Mary."

She smiled brightly, setting the plate down. "Well I'm glad you like it so much. I've got more coming out. I cooked some corn, made so mashed potatoes, have some greens." Mary explained to them as she walked back into the kitchen.

It took a few trips for her before she finally could sit down at the table with the two. "Alright, dig in." Mary said, taking her knife and fork, cutting into the turkey and scooping up a little bit of everything.

The dinner that they had all together was nice. Lots of laughter, lots of compliments, complete joy filled the room between Miriam and Mary, although Robert was most of the time quiet. After dinner, Miriam decided to go play with her doll in the living room while Mary and Robert were in the kitchen, cleaning the dishes.

While they were in there, Robert remained quiet, lost in his thoughts as he kept trying to shake it off. It didn't take too long though for Mary to see something was bothering him.

"You've been awfully quiet this evening...is there something wrong?" Mary asked him, continuing to wash the dishes.

"No." Robert said vaguely, not wanting to get into what was bothering him.

"You sure?" She said softly, looking at him. "You seem like you're thinking really hard about something."

"Don't worry about it." Robert said to her, trying to avoid explaining his thoughts.

Eventually, Mary let out a quiet sigh before setting her dish down, turning toward Robert.

"You know if something is troubling you, you can te-" Mary began to say to him.

"Drop it." Robert said harshly, looking at her for a few quick seconds before he finally set his plate down, shaking his head. "Just forget it...I'm going to bed." He said, leaving the kitchen and walking upstairs.

Mary was shocked by the way Robert reacted, considering it wasn't normal for Robert to be this way.

Miriam heard the commotion from the living room, looking at Mary. "Is papa upset about something?" She said with a concerned voice.

Mary heard Miriam and shook her head. "Don't worry about it dear. He just needs some time to himself."

Chapter IX

Robert currently laid in Mary's bed upstairs, his eyes closed as he tried sleeping. He didn't mean to snap at Mary, but considering his thoughts were getting to him, it was bound to happen. As he attempted to sleep, he soon felt something lay next to him, which interrupted his slumber. He opened his eyes and turned to look and see if it was Mary.

Of course, he was right in this situation. Mary was in her nightgown, having crawled in bed with Robert, getting cozy. Once he saw it was Mary, he returned back to his previous position, his back facing her. Still trying to avoid breaking the news to Mary, he soon felt her arms around his stomach, her body soon pressing against his back.

"What's going on with you? You're usually not like this." She said softly, resting her head against his back.

"I don't know Mary...I don't know." Robert said quietly, his eyes still closed.

"I feel like you do know Robert." Mary finally said. "I just feel like you don't want to tell me what you're thinking of."

He heard what she said, but didn't reply to it. The only thing he did was sit in silence with his eyes closed, trying to fall into slumber.

"You know I'm here if you want to tell me what's bothering you. I think it'd be healthy if you did though because you won't get any sleep with you thinking about whatever you're thinking. I know from experience." Mary quietly said, now closing her eyes as she rested her head against his back.

Robert listened to what she was saying before he let out a quiet sigh, trying to think about how he would explain his thoughts to her. Eventually, he decided to be straightforward with her.

"You know why I decided to move to Lancaster County?" He asked Mary quietly.

She merely shook her head against his back, indicating that she didn't know why he moved here. "Aside from finding a new home, no I don't."

Robert listened to what she had to say before he continued. "I left my previous home because my wife walked out on Miriam and I."

When Mary heard this, her eyes opened up and she sat up, looking down at him. "What? That's horrible! Why would she do that?"

Once Mary sat up, Robert turned so that he was laying on his back, now looking up at her. "To be honest...maybe I married the wrong person. She just...everything seemed fine to me. She was a good mother, I was a good father, we lived a happy life, but then one day..." He said before stopping, thinking back to that day before telling Mary what happened.

"Sara?" He called out, looking around his home. "Where are you?"

While he walked around the house, Miriam watched him, not understanding what was going on. "Papa? What's going on?"

"I can't find mom. She's gone." Robert said, his tone being a little more scared. "Maybe she left something saying where she went. Yeah...she leaves notes."

"Maybe...I'll help you try and find something" Miriam said, getting off of the couch before walking around their home, trying find anything that could lead to the mystery of where Robert's wife went.

Eventually, Miriam found a note that had fallen on the side of the bed. "Papa!" She called out. "I found a note!"

Robert immediately ran into the room, seeing the note in Miriam's hand. He took the note from her and began reading it. Although the hope he had on his expression when he found the note soon faded the more he continued to read it. In fact, he soon had become emotionless from what was written on the note.

"What does it say papa?" Miriam asked, looking up at him.

Robert finished reading the note, looking down at Miriam before folding the note in half, tucking it into his pocket. "Don't worry about it sweetheart. I think though...we need to move away from this county."

When Miriam heard this, she was completely confused. "Why? Why do we need to move?"

He heard her before he picked her up, looking around the house one last time. "Because I think we will find somewhere else that'll be better for the both of us."

"We basically left the county with nothing but the clothes on our back. I couldn't stand living in the same county as her and live in a house that we lived in together." Robert said quietly, looking at Mary as he finished explaining his story. "Would you stay in the same place if you found out your love left you and your child for someone else?"

When Mary heard this, she let out a depressed sigh. "No...I don't think I would." She said quietly. "Is that what's been on your mind today?"

Robert heard her before nodding softly. "I've been thinking about it for a long time now...I've wanted to move onto the next step in our relationship, but...I fear that something would happen again...I fear the odds of you walking out on us."

Once Robert said that, Mary spoke up in a more serious tone. "Robert...look at me."

Robert did as told and look into her eyes, seeing what she would say.

"I would never do that...ever in my life." Mary said, looking at him as she gently rested her hand on his cheek. "I wouldn't do something to hurt you and Miriam...I love you both, with all my heart." She said to him before she gently kissed him, breaking it soon after before resting her head on his chest. "You don't need to worry about me every walking out on you two...I care about you two so much that my heart aches. I wouldn't even think about walking out on you two."

When Robert heard this, he let out a relieved sigh, his arms wrapping around her and hugging her against him. "I love you so much Mary..."

"I love you too Robert..."

THE END

ROLLING HILLS

SHELLY MCDONALD

I drove by an old torn up sign that read "Sugar Grove, Pennsylvania: Population 566." I turned down two side streets and made a left on Trout Avenue before I found a beautiful yellow cottage that sat on Danbury Lane; outside I saw the lawns were freshly manicured and flower pots with garden gnomes took up the empty space. There were vines growing up the cottage and there was a small swing that sat by an old oak tree. I looked up at the sky and saw the sun beginning to set over the hills. I looked over at the neighboring farms and saw cows grazing in the fields nearby. I closed my eyes and listened to the animals chattering about. Other than that, silence filled the air.

I didn't come to this small town to find a cowboy, I came here because I lack emotion. I feel that has to do with a certain woman. Although, one could think the emotions forming inside me was the start of a new relationship. I was both anxious and excited except those feelings were about finding my birth mother. I slaved many late night hours working as a waitress at a small diner making trash for tips. I was grateful for the hard work because it prepared me for college. I aced my way through grad school and ended up landing a job at the LA Times. I was pretty much the paper boy but it was something. It was all that work that got me to where I am today. I skipped any romantic entanglements because I was determined to hunt this woman down and that is hard enough because she comes from a community that doesn't use technology. Lately, I had been feeling lonely. Most of my friends had gotten married and had children by now. I was a lost cause, I guess. I chose the thrill of a career over romance and diapers. I put off my search until recently because it made me feel weak. My only thoughts were about school and work. In order to be great, I needed to shut off my feelings. That was until I landed this job and my boss told me I'm like an onion and not in a good way. The layers are apparently thick and under ripe. He told me to take a vacation and find true emotion.

I walked through the door expecting the cottage to be full of floral arrangements, but I was welcomed by a small kitchen that was connected to the living room. The walls were painted a sky blue and trimmed in white. The pictures on the wall were of sunflowers and honeybees. I saw a small white couch and a small blue chair that faced a television set. A small table, sat between the two chairs, contained a sunflower shaped lamp. A blanket hung over the chair appeared well worn from many years of use. A small dining room table separated the two rooms. At the back of the cottage was a large bedroom. The room held a king size feather bed with all white linen, a large chest of drawers holding a large mirror. In front of the mirror were empty storage containers that were to be filled with my belongings. I glanced at the paintings that hung on the wall. Most of the paintings throughout the house were of beautiful sceneries.

My stomach started grumbling so I headed back towards the kitchen. I was scrounging through the cabinets when I noticed it had been stocked with groceries. A note hung on the fridge from the owners that my assistant had called and arranged for them. I reached for an apple and checked my email. I sent a short message to my boss before I called Rhonda and thanked her for the kind gestures.

It was almost 7 pm and that apple didn't curb my hunger so I decided to look through the contents of the kitchen. Pasta always sounded good and with all the Italian ingredients I saw I decided to whip something easy up. I pulled out some fresh basil, a few Roma tomatoes, a bunch of linguini pasta, and a splash of olive oil. She ended up making Tomato Basil Pasta. I grabbed the remote and sat down at the table and searched the movies on television. I found nothing and opted for classical music and enjoyed the melodies. It cleared my head of all that useless inner babble that seemed to cloud my mind. I was looking out the window and I saw 3 younger kids riding their bikes as an older walked behind them. The older one was reading a book as she walked. She kept stumbling because her mind was obviously in a far off land.

The next day I headed into town to stake out the local bakery. I parked across the street from the bakery. When I stepped in front of the building and took the site in I saw a historical sign that read, "Amish Bakery founded in 1848 by Tobias Hochstetler. The structure was crafted out of natural wood and the window panes had flower boxes carved into them. The word "Bakery" was crafted out of white wooden blocks and plastered on the side of the building. There were fresh flowers in the boxes and the lawn was beautifully tailored. I liked the wooden picnic tables that sat on the front lawn for those who wanted to enjoy the fresh outdoors.

However, I smelled treats baking indoors and that was where I wanted to be. I smelled various bread baking in the large cast iron ovens. Another whiff told me that stew was simmering in pots on the stove in the back. I found a small table in the back. I looked around for a plug remembering Amish had no power which meant no plugs.

I was grateful for my two battery banks or writing was going to be a drag. I was looking around when I noticed the tables each contained a simple vase with a small bouquet of fresh wildflowers sat in the center of each simple table cloth; silverware was already placed out on each table, they were neatly tucked into their napkins. The tables looked hand carved and the decoration that hung appeared homemade. A large quilt was mounted on the wall and it took my breath away. Each stitch was hand stitched by the women of this community. Each block contained a little something from its artist. The squares were beautifully stitched together into one large quilt and presented to the Hochstetler's.

I took notice that people were walking through the doors and taking seats at various tables. The female patrons were dressed in calf length dresses that were of a solid color. Some of the dresses were eggplant in color, but most blues and greens. The women I noticed wore black bonnets over a white prayer cap. They paired their outfit with a pair of black boots. I noticed the men wore light colored shirts and dark pants. They had suspenders that held their pants up. I didn't see a single speck of metal on a single person. When the men entered the bakery they removed their hats and placed them on a rack at the front of the establishment.

It was only a matter of time before the place was almost full. I couldn't figure it out but there was something strange. I finally figured it out the strange thing was called silence. I was in an extremely busy establishment and there wasn't commotion coming from the kitchen or in the dining area. Everyone appeared to be either being working as a team or speaking in hushed tones. The employee's smiles appeared genuine as they greeted each table. I was amazed at how different service was compared to back in the city where people were shouting and their children were climbing over the tables. People always complain about their food in a city.

The waiter came up to my table and greeted me as he did the others. He too was dressed in plain fashion. I looked past his clothes and right into his sea green eyes. I noticed his hair was cut into a shaggy style and his front tooth was slightly out of line. His skin held a golden hue from long hours of working in the sun. He cleared his throat reminding me that he was standing in front of me.

"Hello My name is Abram and I'll be taking your order this morning, are you ready to order?" He repeated his question.

I nervously mumbled something about a breakfast puff, a banana, and a cup of coffee; managing to keep my head averted so that he wouldn't see the color forming its way onto my cheeks. He nodded as he stepped away.

I groaned in embarrassment as I took my simple black laptop from its well-worn bag. I started writing an article on school bus safety while I waited for my order. My boss must really hate me if I'm writing articles on bus safety. Apparently, bus drivers forgot there was such a thing because there has been a rise in bus accidents. I looked over my laptop and noticed some of the other patrons spoke quietly amongst one another, but when the food came they said a word of prayer and ate in total silence.

Abram brought my meal and asked, "Is there anything else I can do for you?"

I thought of many things he could do for me but instead replied with a curt "no thank you".

I glanced back and watched him walk away. I found that the service staff never left the front of the business. They stood at a podium and waited for tables that needed to be serviced. If a patron looked up the waiter was immediately there. No food was sent back and as the patrons left they all thanked the chef in German. I learned "denki" meant thank you and was pronounced "den-gee." Every single table wished to speak with the baker. At first, it struck me as an odd gesture but soon I realized the admiration these people had for this family.

I continued returning to the bakery every day for the next few weeks. I became fast friends with Hannah the female waitress and learned that 6-year-old Mary helped prepare meals when she was not in school. I speak with Abram when he comes by my table. He often gave me his million dollar smile and a quick wave before he went into the kitchen. Sometimes he stopped and chatted with me for a moment, so today when he did she wasn't nervous or scared.

"Hello Annabelle, Have you written any new articles lately?"

"I've written a couple here and there but nothing concrete. Thank you for asking."

"I was wondering if you had any plans tomorrow. I'd like to take you on a picnic."

I noticed his cheeks turn red. Wow.

I sat there frozen in my chair for a moment. I cleared my throat before speaking.

"I'd love too," I responded shyly.

Wildflower

The next day I was busy throwing clothes around the large bedroom so it didn't strike me as odd when I glanced around; a bra hanging from the ceiling fan and a sock fell from the lamp onto the wooden floor. I sighed and decided on a new outfit instead. I drove to a local boutique and bought a pair of capris, solid lavender top, and a white cardigan sweater. "This outfit will look super cute with the white low top sneakers I brought with me," I thought to myself. I pulled my cell phone from my bag and located the GPS app. I looked for a place to eat. I finally found something couldn't find my way back. I drove around for a while and eventually lost cell reception. I accidentally turned left instead of right and went up a hill where I hoped it would loop around but, it didn't instead the road just kept winding around. I wasn't able to turn around or I would have, so I continued driving until finally, I discovered a road that led to the main road. I screamed and yelled at the stupid reception in this little town but I drove another 10 miles before my GPS finally said turn right here and your destination is on the left. I growled at my phone before parking in front of the cottage. I was way behind on schedule. Abram was due soon and may have even left his home already.

I was finishing up my final touches when I heard trotting coming from down the road. I didn't want to seem eager so I left the screen door closed and sat on the couch to read a book. I opened the blinds up so I could see as he got closer. I felt the butterflies begin to swarm in my stomach as I watched the set of American Standardbred horses climb the final hill. I saw a green wagon trailing behind two horses. It was an open two-seater wagon, and even I knew that was more for romantic social calls. The butterflies turned up a notch. I stood and fixed a few strands of hair and checked my breath. I hadn't been on many dates in my life but I had a feeling this one was going to be life altering.

Abram helped me into his wagon and asked if I felt comfortable? Of course, I wasn't, but I'd never let him know that. The seat was hard and moved when I moved. The swaying of the moving wagon caused me to grip the side. Eventually, I got used to the motion and my heart stilled. The brisk northern breeze cooled my flushed face. The fresh air was inviting and it smelled sweet and of freshly cut grass. I had noticed the handcrafted bales of straw, and I was curious about how long it takes for them to do the whole field. I was seated next to someone who would actually answer me with an honest answer.

"Hey Abram, how long do it take to make the bales of straw?"

He spoke with a smile in his voice. "It takes one man many hours hacking the tall grass with a scythe but other farmers often pitch in and help one another. Some help even when they're unable to because they are gracious and kind individuals."

Abram called those individuals God's disciples. I stared at this man in awe. He was such a kind-hearted man. I loved hearing him praise his community like he did because whether he knew it or not he was one of those disciples. His story reminded me of the weeks I sat at the bakery and watched the Hochstetler's as they prepared each dish with joy and hard work. I realized then that the Hochstetler's were also disciples of God. I took a deep breath in enjoying the smell of freshly cut straw mixed with Abram's scent. He seemed to notice my hearty attempt at enjoying the scent of the countryside but didn't notice her feeble attempt at scooting closer. Abram drew in a deep breath and agreed the air was nice. Perhaps he too smelled the countryside mixed with the scent of her instead.

"Have you worked at the dairy farm you were telling me about?" I asked curiously.

"No I haven't, I will start back again tomorrow so I won't see you again until the weekend. I only work in the bakery when work isn't available elsewhere." He stated

A few moments later we pulled into a meadow filled with Eastern Daisies, Bearded Beggar sticks, swamp lilies, Bulbous Buttercups and Black-Eye Susan's. It was full of colors. I saw reds and greens with bursts of yellow and blues. In the center of the white Elderberry and Meadow Rue sat a colorful quilt with a hand woven picnic basket on top. I looked around and saw grasshoppers jumping around and blue and yellow butterflies danced through the sky. Blue birds sat on branches twittering about. I still couldn't believe it was quiet enough to capture moments like this one.

"Oh Abram, it's beautiful!" I cried

"I'm glad you like it. I wanted to find a place where I could get to know you." He confessed.

I laced our hands together and we walked towards the quilt. I brushed my hands along the flowers. I stopped to smell a few; I fell down when a lady bug tickled my nose. I stayed there in that spot and looked up at the sky. What was I doing? I was busy falling in love and I forgot about my mission to find Ruth Hershberger. For now, I was going to enjoy this but I needed to use the weekdays to find out how to get in touch with Ruth.

I stood up and I continued to look around. I took everything in because I wanted to remember this day for the rest of my life. I saw his green buggy on the hillside, the cedar, and the pine trees swaying in the distance. I saw butterflies and dragonflies dancing through the sky. I watched the grasshoppers jump from flower the flower. A laugh escaped my mouth as I twirled around like a child. I felt like I had the world at the tip of my fingers and it's all because of Abram. He talked with me and he listened to me. He paid full attention when I spoke. He never strayed from our conversations, and he never looked bored. He filled me with happiness and he made me feel special.

I walked over to the quilt and sat beside Abram. Together we talked about our hopes and dreams. I picked up a carrot and took a bite before asking him

"Are you happy where you are in life because I feel really lost?"

"I was lost for some time but I prayed that one day I would figure out what I wanted and I found it. I want to open my own furniture store. Why do you feel lost "liebchen"? He asked.

My eyes got teary and I finally told him the truth.

"I came to Sugar Grove in search of a woman. I'm using you the history of your family's bakery as my cover up. I'm trying to locate an Amish woman named Ruth Hershberger. I have some urgent information I need to discuss with her. She may be the woman who gave birth to me."

Abram pulled me into his arms and kissed my head. I melted into his warm embrace, he held me like that until I felt him shifting his body.

Abram laid his body down beside me and looked me in the eyes before he spoke.

"I promise that I'll help you in any way that I can."

"I know you will," Annabelle said truly believing his words.

Abram and I watched the sunset together. Our fingers danced together on the quilt. There were moments of silence but they were filled with laughter. Abram always knew when my mind began wandering. He always attempted to pull me back and I was thankful for the distraction. I saw the stars form in the sky and knew my night was drawing to an end.

"Do you write books? Abram asked me curiously.

"I haven't thought writing books lately but it was a dream of mine growing up," I confessed.

"Do you make things for entertainment or just tools and furniture?" I asked

"You called me something earlier, what was it again?" I asked

"I called you liebchen" he blushed.

What does liebchen mean? I inquired

"It means my love" he spoke confidently.

"Liebchen sounds better than my love if you ask me," I admitted.

I learned he wanted to work with animals and wished one day to be a veterinarian, but he understood that he couldn't afford school. He looked at the sky and announced it was time to start heading home. The buggy ride home was silent but in a good way. The ride home Annabelle could see fireflies lighting up the sky and she could hear crickets chirping in the night. This night felt too good to be true. It felt absolutely bewitching. When they made it to her cottage they heard an owl hooting nearby. Annabelle giggled and confessed she wasn't used to such beautiful noises. She was used to horns honking, sirens blaring, and the usual city noises. She started to enjoy looking up and seeing the constellations in the sky and hearing the animals and insects talk in the night. It felt like a whole other universe out here. Abram pulled up to the little yellow cottage on Danbury Lane and walked me to the door. He looked a little nervous before he finally spoke up.

"Would you like to attend Sunday Worship with my family? It is always nice to listen to the bishop tell tales about "Herr Gott."

"Yes, I would love to join your family on Sunday." I eagerly responded.

"Perhaps you will see Ruth there." He spoke confidently.

"Perhaps I will."

Kiss Me

The week was long and brutal. I continued going to the bakery even though I knew Abram wouldn't be there. I managed to write send an article in and prayed it would hold over until I discovered the actual story I was searching for. I was glad Abram wasn't here because could focus on finding Ruth. I looked through the local phone book and found a Hershberger family lived in Sugar Grove. Their address was close by but I could feel myself cowering down. I also didn't want to march up to Ruth and say "hi might it possible that you carried a child 22 years?" I learned enough to know that the Amish were close knit and they weren't keen on outsiders meddling in their business.

I woke up early Sunday morning and took a bubble bath. I was daydreaming about spending the day with the Hochstetler's and learning about the Amish community that I didn't hear knocking on the door. I was in the middle of daydreaming when I heard a noise again. This time I drained the water and climbed out of the tub. I was putting my robe on when I heard my name being called.

"Annabelle, are you in there?" said a deep male voice.

I recognized that voice but I wasn't dressed to meet him at the door. I stood behind the closed door and answered back.

"Abram is that you?" I asked a little nervous

The last time I looked at the clock it had been 6 am. Who would be here so early?

"Yes, it is Abram are you alright?" He sounded scared.

"I just got out of the shower, I'm going to unlock the doors and go back to my room. Count to 60 and then you can come in." I said awkwardly

Abram busted out laughing and then I heard his faint counting. I ran to the back of the cottage and slammed the door closed. I grabbed my dress off of the hanger and threw it over top of me. I started pulling curlers from my hair when I heard water running in the kitchen. I was curious about that but opted to put on my shoes and fix my hair instead.

Abram helped me into the buggy. We trotted the three miles to his family farm and picked up his sisters Hannah and Mary. The girls looked a little flustered but neither said a word at first. Hannah broke the silence.

"Grosseldre and Maemm rode with Daed to the Yoder bauereie. "

Mary apologized when she interrupted her sister but she saw Annabelle's uncomfortable shifting.

"Hannah our guest doesn't speak Pennsylvania Dutch perhaps you should use Englisch."

Hannah's faced reddened before she apologized.

"Our grandparents rode with our parents to the Yoder Farm so we don't need to pick them up this morning."

"Mary that was kind of you to include Annabelle into the conversation, Herr Gott is smiling down on you for your acts of kindness." The young child's wise older brother acknowledged.

The buggy pulled onto a large farm and parked next to the other rows of wagons. The farm was beautifully maintained. She had noticed the clothes line pulley first, they were empty today. There are usually animals roaming about but today they were confined to the barn. Worship was held on that warm summer morning because there were 200 people that showed up to hear the bishop speak. After he finished speaking children began playing a game in a nearby field. Men helped with farm work as the women prepared the covered dishes. I saw the elderly in chairs and gossiping about the latest news.

The food tasted amazing but I enjoyed wandering around and meeting new people. I was so curious about their lifestyle so I excused myself to take a deeper look. I walked into the big red barn and walked past rows of cows, sheep, and horses. Occasionally I'd pick up some straw and feed an animal. She walked by a pen of baby pigs and melted. They were oinking and oinking. I left the barn and walked towards a tree covered area that separated the farm from the fields. I stumbled upon deer drinking from in a stream and fish skipping in the water. I saw spider webs with dew on them spread across some blackberry bushes. I pulled out my phone and captured the rare moments of beauty.

I was walking back to the others when I saw a woman who looked vaguely familiar. She was helping a small child fix their clothes near the outhouse. I waited until the child ran off before trying to speak with the woman. Maybe she knows Ruth or perhaps she is Ruth. There was something that was pulling me in the direction of that woman. I was about to greet her but she took one look at me and turned and walked away.

The pain felt was unimaginative. My guts hurt and I felt couldn't breathe, I looked for the only one who knew my secret.

"Abram, I am so sorry, but do you think you could take me home? I'm not feeling well." I asked teary eyed.

"I need to let my parents know but I'll meet you at the buggy." He said while walking towards his father.

Abram told his parents that he had to take me home because I was feeling ill. I looked at the row of buggies and was extremely lost. I found Abrams two horses and climbed into the buggy behind them. She was prepared to wait because she knew he was speaking with his family. I leaned forward and saw a tall gorgeous figured getting closer, so I stuck my head out and waved. He bellowed a deep laugh.

"Annabelle that's the wrong buggy Annabelle laughed so hard, but she swore those were his horses. She even fed them saved carrots from her meal.

When we got to my cottage Abram could feel I needed to talk so he asked if I'd like to take a walk. We were walking on the dirt road for a little while before he pulled me onto a walking trail. As we walked the trail Abram took my hand before speaking.

"What happened today at the Yoder farm?"

"I tried to speak to this woman who looked familiar, but she ran away."

I know it sounds childish but I believe it was Ruth.

We walked and talked for a while before Abram spotted a stream. He found a large leaf and made a bowl out of it so that we could enjoy the water. We were walking again this time he took her with confidence and kissed it. We walked for a long time before I asked,

"Are we walking to my home in LA?"

"Come we will rest before we head back to your house," Abraham laughed.

He was used to long hours of walking but he understood that she wasn't accustomed to it.

We walked into a hay field where they sat and rested while they talked. I pulled a piece of straw lose and gathered the courage to see where this relationship was going.

"Have you ever been in love?" I asked timidly

Abram smiled like he was just pondering the topic himself.

"Yes, I have been in love. This woman brightens the sky when she steps into the sunlight. She lights up a room when she walks in with a smile on her face. I hear her heart beats and my world feels absolute. She walks barefoot in the sand and has skin the color of caramel. Her eyes are the color of storm clouds on a hot summer's day. Her lips look like ripe cherries ready for tasting. Abram picked up his queen and placed her on his lap. He kissed me with more passion than I thought possible. He pulled me closer and continued dancing his tongue around in my mouth. I moaned and sank into his embrace. He held me tightly and deepened the kiss. Eventually, he pulled away and kissed my nose before he spoke again.

"Annabelle Michaels, I love you more than I ever thought possible. I'd rather die a lonely man before I'd ever give you up."

We had better start back before it gets too late. I have to work in the morning and you need to find Ruth.

Deception

The next morning I woke up feeling fresh and determined. I decided to take matters into my own hands. I am going to the Hershberger farm and meet this family. I pulled out a cookbook from the cabinet. I decided to make a chicken casserole to show respect for their family. It took me a few hours to get things together and it was almost lunch time. I loaded the rental car and drove to the address I found the other day.

I pulled up to the farm and knocked on the door. The paint was peeling from the wood and the hinges were rusted. There was a large run-down barn behind the house and there was a fenced off area on one side of the house. I knocked again and shouted a greeting. An elderly woman came to the door; she spoke little English and told me to go around back.

Annabelle walked over to the fenced area and shouted

"Hello is anyone here?"

I heard the woman talking to a man in hushed tones but the man turned and walked away, but not before I could see tension rise in his shoulders.

I took a deep breath and she walked up to the woman I saw the other day.

"Good Afternoon, I am Annabelle Michaels and I work with the LA times. I'd like to write a story on your dairy farm if that is ok with you. We want to determine if there is a large difference in the way milk is produced."

The woman chuckled before responding

"I know you came here because you want to know if you're my boppli. I know you want to know if I am your Maemm."

The woman interrupted Annabelle before she could speak. She took my arm and led me to where she was working. Together we talked and pulled weeds from her garden. She naturally chastised me when I was rushed.

"Ruth, didn't you want me for a child?" I dejectedly asked

All these questions started to form in my mind but right when I was about to ask with full confidence I looked up and I saw that golden hair that caught my eye my first day in this town.

I couldn't believe it Abram knew Ruth all along. I had to know why he didn't tell me but right now I just wanted him to know that I now know his secret.

I walked over to him and asked to speak with him alone. He said he needed to finish his shift and he would come to the cottage so we could talk.

I drove the 3 miles back to the cottage in tears, I had learned who Ruth was, and I learned Abram was manipulative and he kept things from those he loved. Neither obviously loved me or cared for me or they would have been honest from the start.

I curled up on the couch waiting to hear from the airlines. I was booking a ticket and getting out of this small town. I was watching reruns on TV when there was a faint knock on the door. I opened the door and there standing was not Abram but Ruth; her birth mother was standing right in her doorway. It was the one thing I always wanted and often dreamed of. I didn't care if I had the perfect man or the comfiest shoes. I just wanted to be accepted by the woman who gave up on me.

I invited Ruth in and listened to her tale that began 23 years ago. I learned my dad was a fisherman and my parents met when my dad delivered fish to the local market. He would often purchase jam from her mom's fruit stand and one time he bought all her jam. He stopped by each summer for three years before her mom finally grew the courage to leave her roots and locate the man that filled her soul. My mother found my father and she claimed he was the love of her life but she only had a few short months with him. She felt punished by god when they discovered he had colon cancer. Her mom had just discovered she was pregnant with Annabelle when her father told her the news. My father stayed with my mom for the first 2 months but when he died my mother was forced to live in a women's shelter until she gave birth. She put me up for adoption and when I was adopted Ruth moved back to her parents and joined the Amish church.

Ruth admitted that she never mentioned Annabelle until Abram confronted her a few weeks ago. Ruth learned Annabelle was getting impatient and wanted to meet her but Ruth was ashamed that she hid her secret for so long. That was when Ruth told her story to the community and to her husband. He knew of her relationship with Annabelle's father but he was unaware she conceived a child. Annabelle drew in a deep breath and immediately thought of Abram and how hard it must have been to confront Annabelle.

"Annabelle, Darling, do you know what your plans are? Are you playing games with Abram or are you prepared to join the church? Abram isn't going to leave his heritage, he knows what he wants. It's up to you to decide if this is the life for you."

There was a knock on the door and they both knew who it was. My thinking time was up but I was fairly sure I had my answer. I opened the door and ushered him to the swing that faced the hills.

"Abram, how long have you known about her being my mom?"

His shoulders sank then he fell to his knees. I saw tears escape his eyes, but there was no way I was going to let him get away that easily. No matter how much I loved this man, he kept something from important from the person he swore he loved.

"Liebchen, I realized the day that you mentioned your birth mother's name. I won't lie, I knew who she was, but I wanted to make sure it was the right person. I didn't want to accuse someone of something she never did. Once I discovered she was the woman you were searching for I asked her to come to you when she was ready because it's her news to share. I wasn't around then and I don't know much now. I do know that there is much she eager to tell and in time I'm sure she will. We both care deeply about you and are worried you will leave. I'm sorry I kept any information from you, I only did it out of protection."

I looked into his eyes as he faced me and I saw the same as when he told me about God's disciples. He was helping a friend in need, this friend just happened to be my mother.

I hadn't seen real emotion until I saw this man's face. It was full of emotions, guilt mixed with grief and a face stained with tears. He held onto my leg like it was the only thing holding us together. I could turn cold and run away but instead, I dropped to my knees and placed my head on his chest. All I wanted was Abram and Ruth in my life. I looked up and I kissed him hard. I fell into his arms and confessed.

"Abram Thomas Hochstetler "Ich liebe dich" than one could love one's self. I used the Dutch phrase for I love you trying to prove my devotion to his heritage. I think of you daily and I pray for your safety each night. I hold you in my heart where I've held no other. There is no way I would turn and walk away; I want to be a part of your life."

He looked at me and laughed a deep humble laugh and before I could interrupt him he took my hands in his and spoke softly.

"Annabelle Naomi Michaels Hershberger, will you marry me?"

THE WEDDING DRESS

GIGI GROSS

Chapter 1

Gabriela stared at her bank account, willing it to change. There was no way she was down to a hundred and twenty dollars. She wasn't getting paid for another three days! Even when she did get paid, a majority of it would get eaten up by her rent and groceries for that week. "Oh no," Gabriela said, laying her head on her arms. She didn't want to think about it, or look at it, or have anything to do with it. Unfortunately, when the problems are in your own life, you cannot exactly run away from them.

Gabriela wanted to call Bryan and get his support. She knew he would have all the verbal support she could want, but he wouldn't be able to loan her any money. His financial situation was just as bad as hers and he made even less money than she did. Once again, Gabby re-evaluated the idea of moving in with Bryan already. It would save them a few hundred bucks a month, and it wasn't so bad. After all, everyone was doing it.

"Maybe then, I would actually have money for a wedding dress," Gabby muttered to herself.

"Having a conversation with yourself again?" Reese asked her.

Gabby quickly minimized her bank account window. "Yes," she replied, trying to put aside her doubts to talk to her sister.

"You're starting to worry me. Turn that frown upside down!" Reese said, coming over and hugging Gabby.

Gabby couldn't help shaking her head and allowing a small smile to form on her lips. "Thanks, Reese." Reese started playing with Gabby's hair, brushing her fingers through its strands. Gabby closed her eyes and sunk into the sensation. It felt so calming to have her sister play with her hair as she had done since she was a little girl.

"Your graduation is in two weeks, isn't it?" Gabby asked, making slow conversation. Reese's hands felt so good.

"Yup! I can't believe I'm actually going to be done with high school. Then, I'm going to college, and that scholarship is seriously a blessing, don't you think?"

Gabby did her best at a nod. "Yes, I don't know how we would do it without that scholarship."

"Do you think Mom and Dad will come to my graduation?" Reese asked in a quiet voice. Gabby was glad she didn't have to look her sister full in the face as she answered.

"I don't know, Reese. Dad might not come because he thinks Mom will be there. Besides, he hasn't really been here for a while. I don't know. Mom might come."

"Do you think she'll bring her terrible boyfriend?"

"I don't know, Reese, but I want you to focus on your success, not on other people. You and only you have been the one responsible for getting yourself through high school. You have studied hard, and this is your time for a reward. I was thinking just you and me could go get ice cream at Scream Cream, maybe not that night but maybe the next if you are too busy partying."

Reese knew that Gabby's money situation was tight, but she just didn't know how tight. Gabby didn't dare let Reese in on the secret. They just needed to get through the summer then Reese would be in college, and Gabby would somehow pull together enough money for just a small wedding.

"When are you going to go dress shopping?" Reese asked after a few moments of silence.

"I don't know, Reese. I will be going soon. Don't worry. You will be invited."

"Yay! You know I am so excited for you! I'll still be able to come home for Thanksgiving or fall break to wherever you guys are, right?"

"Of course, Reese!" Gabby said, finally turning and looking her sister in the eye. "Come here." Even though Reese was eighteen, Gabby was still her big sister at twenty-five. "You will always be my baby," Gabby said, trying to make Reese sit on her lap.

"No!" Reese wailed. "I shall not! I am too old to be sitting on anyone's lap."

"Mmhmm," Gabby smiled mischievously. "I'll just tell that to your striking college boyfriend when you get him."

"Eww!" Reese said. "I'm not going to sit on anyone's lap."

Gabby laughed. "Sure, you say that now. Shall I videotape you saying it and show to you in five years? Come on, help me finish making that garlic bread."

Two days later, Gabby decided to pay a visit to Bryan. They wanted to have their wedding in the middle of August. At this point, they hadn't done anything more than decide it would be held on Bryan's family farm. That decision was based on the fact that it would be a free venue, including free flowers.

"Hey, Baby," Bryan said when Gabby dropped by at dinnertime. "I made something healthy for once. You should be proud of me."

Gabby laughed. "Of course, I'm proud of you. Reese and I rebelliously did not make a salad with our meal last night, so you are doing better than me."

"Come here," Bryan said, pulling her close. He gave her a sweet kiss. When he pulled back, Gabby smiled. This was why she was with him. He always made her feel at home. "Go ahead and sit down. I'll get you a drink in a minute," Bryan commanded.

Gabby took a seat and watched Bryan careen around the kitchen, pouring drinks, draining whole wheat pasta, and preparing their plates. When they finally sat down, Gabby took his hand and listened to Bryan pray. "Thank you, God, for this meal you have given us the resources to have. Please keep giving us all that we need. Amen."

The two began eating, and Gabby finally got up the nerve to bring up the old wedding topic. "Do you think we will even be ready to get married in August? That's only two and a half months away. I'm just worried that we won't have everything ready."

Bryan sighed, but Gabby knew that his frustration was not aimed at her. "I know it's stressful. But, we've almost gotten the rings paid for." Gabby realized at that moment that she forgotten to bring her ring payment that evening.

"Sorry!" Gabby interrupted. "I forgot my payment tonight. I'm getting paid tomorrow, though. I can just give you the money then, right?"

Bryan nodded. "That's fine. I know you're tight too. But, look, we'll have a beautiful meadow, rings, our pastor will come, and gorgeous wildflowers. Maybe we can ask guests to bring a dish. I know it's not conventional," Bryan said in response to Gabby's strange look. "But, maybe they will understand. Feeding so many people can be a few thousand dollars."

"I know," Gabby nodded. "And you paint a beautiful picture. I like the way it sounds. The problem is that. . .I really want to wear a special dress. I've always dreamed of a gorgeous white wedding dress, and I just don't know if I will be able to afford one. I don't want our wedding to just pass by like it's not anything special. I want to look beautiful for you." Gabby's voice cracked with emotion, and she looked down to avoid crying.

Bryan reached over and pat her hand. "I know that it is important to you. It's important to me that you have the wedding just how you want it. But I want you to know that whatever you choose to wear, I will love it." That was when Gabby realized that her yearning to wear such a beautiful gown might not be because she wanted Bryan to think she was beautiful. Maybe she just wanted to feel beautiful for once, not for anyone else but for herself.

Chapter 2

On Saturday, Gabby left Reese sleeping at home in bed to peruse the local flea market. She needed to get Reese a graduation present, but she also didn't have a lot of money to spend on something like that. She had no idea what she wanted to get her sister, but she knew that she liked to read. Perhaps, Gabby could find a few books at a reasonable price.

Gabby was looking at a table of books, holding a couple in her hands. The three books were only twelve dollars altogether, and Gabby thought they would be a great present for Reese right before her last free summer. Gabby looked up, and her eyes fell on a shining white dress hanging on a mannequin the next stall over. Gabby left the three books on the table and walked toward the dress as if in a trance.

Her hand reached up to stroke the fabric. Just as her fingers were going to touch the fabric, Gabby wondered if she should. She looked around to see if anyone was watching her. She saw a small, elderly woman with her eyes trained on her.

"Oh, sorry," Gabby said, stumbling into an apology. "I'm sorry. I didn't know if it was alright to touch, but it's so.. .pretty."

"Go ahead," the woman said in a raspy but friendly voice. "You may touch it." Her smile encouraged Gabby just the bit she needed to have the courage. She turned back to the dress and stroked it. It was soft, almost like silk. The beadwork was amazing, with little detail stitched along the folds of the fabric. The bosom was covered with exquisite beadwork, and the waist came in before flowing out in a long skirt. The train was not overwhelming but still had a presence. It was as though someone had created a wedding gown out of Gabby's imagination.

Gabby's breath caught in her throat. She didn't want to turn away from the beauty. She stealthily scanned the dress for a price tag. Of course, there was not one. That must mean that the dress was handmade and would cost even more.

"Th-thank you," Gabby said, turning away from the dress and nodding to the woman. She took a backward step away from the dress and the woman.

"Are you getting married?" the woman asked, leaning forward encouragingly.

"Yes," Gabby nodded. "But, we don't have a date yet. It will still be a few months." Finally, she shrugged her shoulders and figured she might as well ask how much the dress cost. If she didn't, she would constantly wonder. At least with a number, she could walk away from it without feeling guilty. "How much is the dress?" Gabby nodded toward the wedding dress she had been studying.

The old woman smiled and leaned back. "Oh, that dress doesn't have a price. I'm sure you noticed. It is a beautiful and priceless piece. But," the woman continued speaking before Gabby could turn away. "I will let you wear the gown for free if you promise me one thing."

"What?" Gabby whispered, unable to wait to hear her words.

"You must live out your marriage according to God's will."

"I-uh-oh," Gabby seemed unwilling to respond. "I can wear it. . .for free?"

The woman nodded. "There's a veil that goes with the dress as well, but I must have you promise that your marriage will be uplifting to God. Can you do that?"

"I promise with my whole heart," Gabby said. She couldn't control the smile that spread across her face.

The woman nodded. "Very well. God, our good Lord, will hold you to your word. Now, just give me a moment to gather the dress and package it safely. Do you have a few minutes?"

"Yes, of course!" Gabby could hardly believe her good fortune. "Do you need any help? I could help you."

"That blue bag up there on the shelf, yes, that one. That's the veil. Go ahead and get that down, will you?" Gabby strained up to reach the high shelf, took down the bag, and could not help peering into the bag to examine the veil.

"What do you think?" the woman asked, nodding at the veil.

"It's amazing," Gabby said. The woman carefully took out the veil and used the comb part to place the veil on Gabby's head. She handed Gabby a small hand-mirror, and Gabby nearly cried. She looked like a real bride, not a bride who didn't have any money. Spontaneously, Gabby reached down and hugged the old woman. "Thank you," she sobbed out. The woman patted Gabby's back.

Finally, Gabby carefully folded the veil and put it back in the bag. She then helped the woman take the dress off the mannequin and store it in a garment bag.

"I have one more thing for you," the woman said as Gabby prepared to leave. The woman pulled out a thick book. "I want you to take a look at this. This dress, you see, has a long history. It has made many brides happy on their wedding day, and they all needed it in one way or another. I encourage you to find out about their stories and write your own as well."

Gabby took the thick, leather bound book in the crook of her arm and tried to give the woman one last hug while balancing her packages. "How will I find you again?" Gabby asked.

"I'm always right here," the woman assured her. "Come back after your wedding, and I'll be waiting."

Gabby smiled, thanked the woman one more time, then hurried out of the flea market, forgetting all about Reese's graduation present. The smile could not be wiped off her face. She carefully laid the dress across her backseat and could not help but sing along with every song on the radio. The only thing left to do was try it on. When she reached home, she carried the dress inside and explained the whole story to Reese who at first felt deceived that her sister had gone wedding dress shopping without her.

"I'm going to try it on," Gabby said. "Wait until I'm in it, okay? Don't come in!" Gabby shut the door with her sister outside and changed as carefully as she could into the wedding dress. Gabby could tell the dress had had sleeves at some point. But, it was now a sleeveless dress. The hem was a little long, but Gabby knew she could fix that. Around her waist, the dress fit perfectly. Gabby tucked the veil into place then opened the door with a smile.

"Sis!" Reese said. The smile filling her face was all that Gabby needed to see. "It's perfect isn't it?"

"Yes, it is!" Reese gave Gabby a hug. "I can't believe you are actually getting married!"

"It seems real now."

"It is real," Reese said. "I know Bryan would love you in this dress. I wish he could see it now."

"I know!" Gabby laughed. "But it has to be our secret. "No words to him about it. None, do you hear me?"

Later that night, Bryan came over. He got along well with Reese, and Gabby loved that about him. After all, she might not be Reese's official guardian, but she was Reese's home ever since their parents had started their incessant bickering.

The three were playing a game of Phase 10, and Reese kept smiling randomly at Gabby. "Is something wrong with you?" Bryan asked her. "Or do you two have a cheat going on?"

Both Gabby and Reese laughed. "Nope, we're not cheating," they said in unison.

"Okay, because that denial was totally believable. Come on, I know something is up." Gabby looked at Reese. They both shrugged, but Gabby could not longer keep the news in.

"I got my wedding dress today," Gabby said.

"What?! That's amazing, Gabby. Where is it? Can I see it? Was it expensive?"

"To all of those questions, the answer is no. Besides, the groom is never supposed to see the dress before the wedding day."

"I've got an idea," Bryan said, leaning forward. "Want to get married tomorrow?"

"Sorry," Gabby shook her head. "Pastor is occupied tomorrow. Besides, I'm not ready yet."

"Aw," Bryan visibly drooped. "I guess we should probably wait until we have rings, huh?"

"That would be important!" Gabby said. She gave Bryan a playful kiss and was glad that she did not feel as desperate for a dress as she had that morning.

Chapter 3

Gabby carefully opened the book the woman had given her the day before. In the excitement of trying on the dress and spending time with Bryan, she hadn't thought about it again until she and her sister were leaving church. She hadn't told her sister about the book or how exactly she had gotten the dress, but she had told her enough to be satisfied.

The book appeared to be some sort of journal. On the pages were handwritten notes, some in cursive, some printed, and clearly not all done by the same person. Beside each handwritten note was a picture of a woman wearing the wedding dress. Gabby ran her hands over the first picture. The dress had had sleeves, just as Gabby suspected. The picture looked old, and it was worn around the edges. But it had stayed faithfully in the book. Beside it was a note.

"Teresa Daniels, age twenty-four. Married to Bertram Frantz, age twenty-four, on May 7, 1978. My parents had both died when I was five. I had been living with a family friend since then. The boy I grew up living next to asked me to marry him, but I didn't have any money for a wedding, let alone a beautiful dress. I met this wonderful young woman who loaned me a dress that she had just finished making. She told me to tell my story and live my marriage in a way that would make God pleased with me. I am determined to do just that. My adoptive parents may not have enough money to pay for a wedding, but this wedding dress shows just how much God is looking out for us."

Underneath the note was Teresa Frantz's contact information. In different handwriting was a little note that said she had died in a car accident in 2004. Gabby suddenly felt as though she was holding something very sacred. The dress was only used perhaps once a year, if that, and Gabby hungrily read through each story. Each woman had something to say about how she did not have enough money or something had befallen her. Gabby wondered why their contact information was there. Did they really want someone to talk to them? And what did they want to talk about?

Gabby pictured herself eight years from now with a few small children. She would always remember how she had gotten her wedding dress. What would she say to someone else who was going to use it? Gabby could only smile.

She selected two of the most recent weddings and decided to write to their email addresses. Her message was simple.

"Hi, my name is Gabriela. I'm going to use the wedding dress. I found your information in the book, and I was wondering if you'd like to meet and have a coffee."

Gabriela went to bed at close to two in the morning. "I am so not going to be awake for work in the morning," Gabby said. She had received her payment in her account over the weekend, and Gabby spent a little time that Monday morning paying her bills. It was just as nasty as ever. Even though she had a wedding dress now, she still would not be able to save any money after paying everything necessary. She sighed and shook her head. "It's okay," she told herself.

The workday passed well enough, but Reese was celebrating when she got home because she only had two more exams before she was officially done with school. Gabby spent some of the evening quizzing Reese before she gave herself the luxury of checking her email. She had received a reply.

"It's nice to hear from you, Gabriela. I would love to meet for coffee. How does Wednesday at lunch hour sound? Would it be possible for me to meet you at the Starbucks in Clayton?

Annabel"

Gabriela rejoiced over the email. She couldn't wait to meet this woman and unravel a bit more of the dress mystery.

When it finally came time for her Wednesday lunch hour, Gabby drove as quickly as she could to the Starbucks. She ordered and looked around for Annabel. She finally found her, and the two shook hands in a formal manner.

"I'm so glad you reached out and contacted me," Annabel said. "I wondered if anyone ever would."

Gabby smiled excitedly. "I can't believe the dress was first loaned out in 1978. It still looks so new."

"Well," Annabel surmised. "The sleeves were taken off, and I think some extra beadwork was added."

"Still," Gabby smiled. "It's like I'm wearing a little bit of history."

Annabel laughed. "Yeah, it's magical the way that woman wants to help us. It's like she can just sense the desperation in someone."

"So, what's your story?" Gabby asked, wanting to fill in the blanks Annabel's note had left.

Annabel nodded. "I was eighteen when I got the wedding dress. I know, I was young. I didn't want to get married yet, but my boyfriend had gotten me pregnant. I had just found out a few days before. I had talked to my boyfriend, and he and I decided we would just have a quiet wedding, a justice of the peace deal. I didn't want to do that, but I knew we needed to do something quickly. I didn't want to be one of those boldly pregnant brides. But I was so frustrated with the whole situation, that I had just decided I would wear an old dress. It didn't matter.

"When I saw that wedding dress, though, I couldn't help but be drawn to it. When the woman told me it was free for my use as long as I lived a godly marriage, I couldn't believe my good fortune. We had a justice of the peace wedding, but I was wearing a gorgeously beautiful wedding gown. I will never forget that woman's generosity." Annabel shook her head.

"So, it made your day magical?" Gabriela asked in excitement.

Annabel laughed aloud. "Yes, it sure did. My wedding may not have been what I had imagined it to be when I was fifteen or sixteen, but it was much better than it would have been under the circumstances. Now, I have Gracen, and she's getting close to her second birthday."

"Wow! That's so amazing."

"What's your story?" Annabel leaned forward and listened as Gabriela told her about her all the financial troubles she had had. Gabriela and Annabel continued chatting until the last possible minute.

"I really need to get back to my job," Gabby said, "Or I could lose it. That is definitely not what I need right now. Look, I really enjoyed talking to you. Maybe we could get together again, and I could meet Gracen?"

"I'd like that," Annabel said. "I'll talk to you later."

Chapter 4

Gabriela finally got a reply from the other woman she had contacted about meeting: Brianne. Brianne's story had seemed really tragic, and Gabriela couldn't wait to hear about it from the woman's lips.

After the introductions, Gabriela leaned forward for Brianne's story. "I'm really glad you wanted to talk," Brianne said. "I feel like this dress has created a secret group."

"Have you ever talked to Annabel?" Gabriela asked.

"Annabel. . .Annabel. I don't think so. Was she married after me?"

"I don't remember," Gabriela said. "But I have her number. Maybe we could all three get together or even more brides."

Brianne smiled. "I like the idea. I am definitely willing to contribute. Okay, so here's what happened to me. My problem was not so much a financial one as I read in so many stories. Instead, my problem was a big fire. About five days before the date our wedding was set, some sort of electrical malfunction sparked in our house. My family lost everything. Insurance took care of the problem financially, but the dress I had so carefully picked out months before along with my shoes and veil had been consumed by the fire. Trying to get a dress five days before a wedding is pretty much impossible.

"But, this beautiful old lady performed a miracle. She let me borrow the dress. It was much better than the dress I had originally picked. Better than that, it was ready for the wedding two days early." Brianne shook her head. "I had thought I might need to call off the wedding. I was freaking out. I couldn't even go to work I was so stressed out. I had a few burn marks from escaping the house, but the dress covered them nicely. They can't even be seen in the photos."

"Wow!" Gabby said, soaking in her new friend's story. "Wow." She was silent for a few minutes as Brianne's story sunk in. "Did you know that there have been thirty-three weddings in that dress? I'll be number thirty-four."

"When is your wedding?" Brianne asked.

"It'll be mid-August, right after my sister moves into her college dorm. She's been living with me."

"Would you mind if I rudely invited myself to your wedding?" Brianne smiled.

Gabby laughed. "Of course not. You are welcome. It's going to be a small wedding, and we ask that each guest bring a dish of food, a sort of potluck. We really don't have the money for much more, but I would be honored for you to come."

After meeting the two brides, Gabby wanted to meet more. She kept setting up even more appointments with brides. She had one last meeting planned before her wedding. This meeting took a few weeks to set up. By the time Gabby met her, it was the first day of August.

"What's your story?" Gabby asked impatiently. The question had become one of which she could not wait to ask each new woman. Hallie had been married almost ten years ago.

"My story's probably a bit different from some others," Hallie shook her head. Gabby had agreed to come to her house because Hallie had three young children. Hallie wanted them to be able to play and stay out of their hair while the two women talked. "I was poor. I couldn't buy a wedding dress. That much is as normal as for any of us women."

Gabby nodded, anticipating more.

"My story becomes interesting after I married Mark. Did the lady have you make a promise?"

Gabby nodded. "Yes, I promised that I would live my marriage according to God's will."

Hallie accepted Gabby's words. "Yes, I promised the same thing. At the time, I promised it because it seemed such an easy exchange for the dress. But it wasn't as easy as I thought it would be. The first year of marriage was so difficult. I looked back on the innocence I sported on my wedding day, and I would shake my head. How had I thought I loved Mark?" Hallie was quiet as she remembered. "I was sure that we were going to get a divorce. You see, his family lives on the other side of the country. I know he was really close to them, but he agreed that living here would be the best solution for us.

"But, it was like he had forgotten that. We argued almost every night. I started to hate him. He made me cry so much." Hallie shook her head, and Gabby should see the tears brimming in her eyes. "I started fantasizing about running away and going a place where he wouldn't find me. Then, I remembered my promise. I tried to weasel my way out of it, saying that the fighting was Mark's fault. I blamed him, but I knew I needed to take credit for my part. So, I started serving Mark instead of myself.

"Even when I was tired, I would make dinner. I would clean up without complaint. He noticed after a month, and I felt him become more tender toward me. We were finally able to talk through what had been happening. That was the best day of my life, the day that we finally talked it all through without screaming. I finally slept next to him and felt connected to him again.

"Gabby, that promise is going to be hard to keep. You will probably get angry with your fiance sometimes, but don't walk away. The weak walk away; it's the strong that keep fighting."

Gabby hugged Hallie as a few tears spilled over. "Thank you, Hallie. I needed to hear those words. They were just what I needed." Before Gabby left Hallie's house, she invited her to her wedding. "I know it is only two weeks, but if you think you can come, I would really like it. Don't be shy about bringing your husband and children."

Chapter 5

On the day of her wedding, Gabby carefully donned the dress. It was to be a simple ceremony. Only her sister would stand beside her. Bryan was having his best friend stand beside him. At that moment nothing felt simple about Gabby as she waited for Reese to calmly do up the back.

"I can't believe it's really the day," Gabby said.

Reese smiled. "Yeah, I'm pretty sure I'm having the most exciting first weekend home from college out of all of my friends." Of course, her statement made Gabby start asking about all of Reese's new friends. She had to make sure that her baby sister was doing well and having fun in college.

"Is it done?" Gabby asked.

Reese nodded. "It's done. You're all ready."

"Well, not completely," Gabby said. "I look fine, but I feel a bit nervous about walking down that aisle."

"Why?" Reese asked. "Are you unsure about Bryan?"

"No," Gabby shook her head. "I know he is perfect for me, well, as perfect a fit as someone can be with my rather strange personality."

Reese laughed. "Then, what is making you nervous?"

"I guess it just hit me that this is a lifelong commitment. I love Bryan, and I just don't want anything to go wrong. What if we start living together, and he does annoying things that get on my nerves?"

"Like what?"

"Like leave his socks on the bed."

"Then tell him to take his socks off," Reese shrugged. "It's not that hard. Look, if you love him and you know that for sure, then you just have to go through the bad stuff and remember that. Then you'll get to the good times, and it'll be all worth it."

"Alright, my sister the wise," Gabby smiled. "What time is it?"

Reese looked at her phone. "We still have thirty minutes."

"What a long thirty minutes that'll be!" Gabby sighed, carefully sitting in her dress.

Reese laughed aloud. "I thought you just said you were nervous to do it, and now you can't wait to go down the aisle."

Gabriela laughed with her sister. "When you get to this point, I will be right by your side and remind you of everything you just said. Meanwhile, you'll just be like. No, I'm nervous! Let me be nervous by myself!"

Gabriela's friend Erica burst into the bedroom just then. "Hey! Wow, Gabby! You look so amazing!" Erica was the unofficial photographer. She had a professional camera and had done some photo shoots. A free photographer was her wedding gift to her friend. "Look, we don't have a lot of time, but I wanted to get a few pictures of just you in all your bridal beauty, then maybe a few with Reese. Hey, Reese! How are you?" Erica said in one breath.

Gabby laughed. "Oh, Erica, I knew there was a good reason we were friends." Erica took all the photos she wanted with Gabby sitting, standing, lounging, smiling, and serious.

"Alright, Reese, get in there with your sister." After a few more shots, Erica hovered over to the door. "Alright, I believe we have five minutes before your little flower girl will start her march. Let's get you safely down these stairs."

Gabby carefully maneuvered the stairs with the help of her sister and friend. The stairs were not very wide and definitely not prepared to have brides tramping up and down them. She finally stood by the back doors.

"Ready?" Reese asked.

Because Gabby had decided against having their estranged father walking her down the aisle, Reese would be walking right beside her.

"I think so," Gabby answered. "But ask me again in a minute, and I might have a different answer."

"You've got this, Sis."

"Thanks."

Erica reappeared as the music started to assist the flower girl on her way. Next went the ringbearer. After that came Gabby and Reese. It was a simple, small wedding, just as Gabby had dreamed it. Best of all was Bryan's face when she came through the doors of the back of the farmhouse.

His smile was genuine and delighted, and Gabby looked only at him as Reese guided her steps down the aisle. When she reached the altar, she placed her hands in Bryan's, smiling into his eyes and wondering how she had ever doubted her decision to marry him.

"I love you," she whispered as the pastor was talking to them. He mouthed the words back and gave her hands a squeeze. Suddenly, the ceremony, including a candle lighting, a song sung by a friend, and a short talk from the pastor seemed all too long to Gabby. After what seemed an eternity, the words she had wanted to hear for so long pierced her thoughts.

"You may now kiss the bride."

Gabby kissed Bryan, leaning into his lips. When they pulled back, Gabby felt the magic of the moment lingering. "You're my husband," she whispered, incredulous.

"And you, my dear, are my wife." Bryan let go of one of her hands, facing the audience. The pastor announced them, and Bryan paused before they started down the aisle. "This is my wife!" he shouted, his pleasure clear as he lifted up their joined hands in victory. Gabby started laughing. Suddenly, a huge cheer rose up from the back of the rows of seats. Gabby looked over and counted five of the former brides that she had met.

"Yes, Gabriela!" They screamed together. While Gabby had not pictured her wedding as loud as a ballgame, she couldn't help laughing aloud.

Bryan carefully led her down the steps, and they entered the old farmhouse. As soon as they were inside, Bryan turned to her and kissed her passionately. "You are the most beautiful bride I have ever seen," he whispered. "And tonight, I will make you mine." Gabby trembled with anticipation, leaning in for another kiss.

A week later, Gabby carefully zipped the wedding dress into the garment bag for the last time. She took out the book and carefully glued in a photo of herself wearing the dress. She smiled at the photo then took up a pen and began writing in her best cursive beside the photo.

"Gabriela Winfox, age twenty-five. Married to Bryan Davis on August 21, 2016. This dress changed my life. Not only did it give me a chance to have the kind of wedding I would never have had on my budget, but it showed me the friendliness and generosity this kind of world doesn't see very often. It made me promise to be a more generous person and to look for opportunities to help others. I didn't have any money for a nice wedding, and my fiance and I feared we would not be able to throw a wedding. Determined to get married, because we knew it was right, I thought I would never have a wedding dress. I was wrong. Please, contact me. I would love to talk to you, and I know that the brides I met would love to talk to you as well. We are in this together."

Gabriela signed her name under her words and closed the book with a solemn thud. "Thank you, God," she said as she loaded the dress, veil, and book into the back of her car. She was on her way to the flea market.

The Golden Amish Pond

Deidra Scott

Chapter One

The sun was just starting to go down below the hills. Sitting at their favorite picnic spot, Lucy Miller closed her eyes and took a deep breath of the sweet spring air. It had now been five years since she and her family moved from Indiana to the new Amish community in Kentucky. Five years, and yet it felt like a lifetime.

"Lucy," The voice of Lucy's boyfriend, Michael, caused Lucy to open her eyes and turn her head in his direction.

Ach, he looked so sweet in the dimming light. Reaching out, he pulled Lucy closer to himself, and whispered, "I guess it's about time we packed up this picnic and headed back home. I'm so stuffed on your fried chicken, I don't think that I could eat another bite."

Lucy smiled to herself. Ever since she and Michael had started courting last year, he had constantly amazed her with his hearty appetite for anything she cooked.

Pulling herself to a standing position, Lucy began to pack up leftover food and put it away in her wicker basket.

"Lucy," She was just about to start folding the picnic blanket when Michael reached out and grabbed his hand in her own, "Lucy," he repeated again, "I want to ask you, I mean, I've been looking for a way..." taking a deep breath, he started again, "Lucy, you've come to be very special to me. I want ya to be my wife. Will you marry me?"

These were the words that Lucy had been waiting her entire life to hear. She had expected him to ask and yet it now felt completely strange and surprising.

"Lucy..." Michael held her hand in his own and stared straight in her eyes, "Do you love me too?"

Did she love him?

"Oh, Michael, yes!" She exclaimed, reaching out to throw her arms around his neck, "Yes, ever so much, yes!"

Michael's handsome face broke out in a wide grin.

Holding him in a hug, Lucy leaned her head against his chest and took a deep breath. This was what was supposed to happen. This was what was right.

Lying alone in the dark that night, Lucy couldn't sleep. Her mind felt like it was running in circles.

When she first met Michael at a young peoples' meeting, he had instantly swept her off her feet. Michael had caught her eye first thing, and had done everything possible to catch her heart.

It only made sense for them to be together. Didn't it?

Sitting up in bed, Lucy took a deep breath and let it out slowly.

Reaching out for a match, she struck it and then carefully lit the lamp that sat on her nightstand.

Pushing aside the quilt her mamm had made her, she pulled herself to her feet and went to the dresser that sat at the end of her bed. Pulling open the top drawer, she gave her black socks a shove to the right, giving her access to the assortment of special papers that she had stored beneath them.

Sorting through the papers, she got quick glimpses of various school awards and birthday cards. At the bottom of the pile, she found it.

A golden ring.

Lifting it up to the light of her lamp, Lucy rolled it around and around between her fingers, treasuring the slick feel and watching it glow in the darkness.

Cody Armstrong.

That name had haunted her for years now. She thought about him constantly, and the promises that they had made to each other.

She had promised Cody that she would one day marry him, and he had promised her the same when he handed her the ring.

Reaching up to wipe away at some tears, Lucy fought back a torrent of old emotions.

Slipping the piece of forbidden jewelry onto her ring finger, Lucy stared at it and took a deep breath. How she wished that she could have some closure and some way to put the past to rest once and for all.

Putting the ring back in its place in the drawer, Lucy tried to blot out the memory of the handsome blonde-haired Cody by thinking of Michael. Try as she might, it was impossible to erase the thoughts of the boy she had loved first.

It was time for her to move on and focus on her life with Michael.

Getting into bed and pulling the quilt over herself, Lucy closed her eyes and reached up to wipe away at the tears that threatened to overtake her.

"God," she whispered into the darkness, "Would you please give me some way to put the past in the past?"

Monday morning came bright and early. Despite her restless night, by seven o'clock, Lucy had already helped her mamm cook a delicious breakfast of fresh scrambled eggs, toast, and bacon, cleaned up the dishes, and was now out helping her daed and little brothers gather eggs in the chicken barn.

Although morning offered a fresh start, Lucy found that the rising of a new day didn't help her to resolve any of her problems. Her mind still felt like it was in a whirlwind, and she was overwhelmed by the troubles she had thought about the night before.

The sound of a truck brought Lucy's father to attention. Hurrying to lay aside some eggs, he glanced out the barn door and called out, "Looks like Tommy Smith is coming to pay us a visit."

Tommy Smith was the Miller's Englischer neighbor. He often gave the Miller family rides into town, or let them use his phone when they needed to make a call.

"Morning, Tommy!" Mr. Miller called out as Tommy came walking into the barn. The older man wore a broad smile on his face.

"Good morning to the Miller family!" He returned as he stopped beside a bag of chicken food, "I got a message for you all this morning. It was from your oldest daughter Rebecca."

Lucy and her brothers quit working so that they could gather around and hear the news about their sister who still lived with her husband in Indiana.

"Rebecca said to tell you that you are a new grandpa!" Tommy announced, "She had a little baby boy. They named him Jacob."

Lucy was overcome by joy at the thought of yet another new baby in the family. She watched as her daed's face broke out in a big grin, and looked down at her beaming little brothers.

"She wanted to know if you could possibly send Lucy up to help her for a few weeks," Tommy continued.

Suddenly, Mr. Miller's face sobered. Looking to his daughter, Lucy could feel him searching her face in uncertainty.

"Ach," he slowly muttered, "I suppose that would be all right. Lucy, do you want to go help your sister?"

Lucy slowly nodded her head, "Sure, Dad."

Turning back to her work, Lucy felt butterflies fill her stomach. Rebecca wasn't the only one still in Indiana. Cody Armstrong was as well.

Chapter Two

Tommy Smith agreed to give Lucy a ride to her sister's house. By Monday afternoon, Lucy had said goodbye, packed her bags, and was on her way to Indiana.

Telling Michael goodbye had been difficult. He hadn't wanted to let her go, and Lucy had been sad to part with him. Having just become engaged, Michael was ready to set a date for their wedding and start planning for their new life together.

While Lucy definitely understood Michael's feelings, the trip to Indiana seemed like an answer to her prayers.

Sitting in the passenger seat of Tommy's truck, Lucy resolved to not only use this trip as an opportunity to help her sister, but also a chance to put the past behind her by sorting through her feelings about Cody.

As the rolling hills of Kentucky slowly gave way to the flat lands of Indiana, Lucy took a deep breath and leaned back against the headrest. Through the open truck window, she let the breeze dance through the lose tendrils of hair that had escaped her black bonnet.

With each mile that they grew closer to Rebecca's house, Lucy felt herself overwhelmed by a torrent of emotions.

She was finally home.

By the time Rebecca's white house came into view, Lucy was practically dancing in her seat. She was so anxious to get out of Tommy's truck, see her sister along with the new baby, and experience whatever might be ahead of her during her short visit to Indiana.

Once Lucy was out of the vehicle and on Rebecca's front porch, she didn't have to wait long to see her sister. Almost as soon as she knocked on the door, she heard her name being called.

"Lucy!" Rebecca's cheerful voice was welcoming her, "Come in, come in!" Swinging the door open, she welcomed Lucy into her house.

"Rebecca!" Lucy grabbed her sister by the arms and smiled up into her tired face, "It's so good to be here!"

"Ach, it so wunderbar-gut to see you!" Rebecca returned as she clasped Lucy's hands in her own, "Oh, sister, it has been too long!"

Looking around the house, Lucy asked, "Where's the baby?"

Rebecca shook her head and laughed, "Little stink is finally asleep. I think he's making it his mission to totally wear me out. He's up all night and then sleeps when I should be working. I truly am glad that you're here, Lucy. I was so afraid daed wouldn't let you come after everything that happened in the past..." Rebecca suddenly sobered, her words bringing a cloud over their once-cheerful visit. Trying to brighten up the mood, Rebecca smiled and announced, "No need to be speaking of that. Those times are over now!"

As Lucy let Rebecca show her some work that needed to be done around the house, she found her sister's words playing over and over again in her mind. Were those times really over? It didn't seem like it. No, as long as Cody Armstrong invaded her thoughts, the past would never really be behind her.

Over the next few days, Lucy stayed busy helping Rebecca around the house. Since the baby was keeping her up at night, Rebecca spent a lot of her time napping and trying to regain her strength. Lucy found herself with chores like washing the dishes, scrubbing floors, doing laundry, and cooking meals for Rebecca and her husband Benji.

Each day, Lucy found herself wondering about Cody. Did he still live in this area? Would she find a chance to see him before her daed called her back home?

On Monday morning, Lucy was preparing to start baking some bread when she realized that Rebecca was out of flour. Rather than wait for Benji to pick up the supplies on his way home from work, Lucy hitched up the buggy and made the short trip into town by herself.

There was something about being out of the house that did Lucy good, and being back on the familiar turf of her childhood put a thrill in her heart.

After stopping by the grocery story and picking up the ingredients she needed, Lucy decided to take the long way back to Rebecca's and instead opted for the road past her old home.

As the large white farmhouse came into view, Lucy felt herself fighting back tears. She had so many good memories of that place. Ach, how she had hated it when her daed had announced they were moving to Kentucky!

Slowing down the horse, Lucy took the chance to soak in every detail of her old home. From the new name on the mailbox and the clothes-line hung up in the yard, it was obvious that a new Amish family now lived there – a fact that brought a bitter-sweet feeling to her heart.

Still creeping down the road in the buggy, Lucy took time to investigate the next house on the road.

The modern two-story brick house looked the same as always. Glancing at the mailbox, Lucy felt her heart give a leap when she saw the name "Armstrong".

Cody's family still lived there.

On a sudden impulse, Lucy led her horse down the short drive to his parent's house and stopped the buggy next to their porch. Getting down from her seat, she made her way to the front door and pushed a button to ring the bell.

As Lucy waited for someone to answer the door, she was suddenly overtaken by nerves. What on earth was she doing? She was an engaged Amish woman – she certainly didn't need to be tracking down an old English boyfriend.

Before Lucy could turn to leave, the door swung open, revealing a handsome young man.

Cody.

She would have recognized him anywhere. Even after five years, he was the same.

His blonde hair was swept back to the side, his blue eyes matching the t-shirt he wore, and his clothes the latest in Englischer fashioned. He looked so good that Lucy felt her heart instantly give a leap, and she wondered if she might faint.

"Lucy..." he said her name slowly as he shook his head, "Wow. It's been so long."

Lucy suddenly felt herself growing bashful. Looking down at the porch, she slowly nodded her head, "Ach, I guess it's been a while."

Stepping out onto the porch in front of her, Cody let out a whistle, "You haven't changed at all. My little childhood sweetheart is still as pretty as ever. Prettier, actually."

Suddenly, he reached out his arms and put them around Lucy, wrapping her up in a tight hug. Something about being back in his embrace felt so good. Lucy closed her eyes, breathing in deeply of his gut-smelling body spray.

Pulling back from her, Cody reached to lift up her chin so that she was staring him in the eyes.

"My gosh, I've missed you," he muttered under his breath.

With each word he spoke, it felt like another piece of Lucy's heart was melting. She wanted to step back into his arms and let him hold her for the rest of her life.

"Why are you here?" Cody asked softly as he ran a finger down her cheek, "Have you moved back?"

Lucy slowly shook her head, her eyes filling with sudden tears, "I'm here helping my sister. Cody, I just had to see you. I had to know..." Suddenly, she was crying uncontrollably. Cody reached out and pulled her toward him, sheltering her and comforting her against him.

Suddenly, their precious moment was interrupted by the ringing of his cell phone.

Letting out a curse, Cody announced, "I have got to go to work." Pulling back from Lucy, he reached down to brush some lose hair out of her eyes, "I want to see you again." Pulling a piece of paper out of his pocket, Cody scribbled out his phone number and handed it to Lucy, "Please, call me tonight. I want to meet up with you when we can truly talk."

Lucy nodded her head. For the first time in five years, it felt like all her conflicting feelings were truly being resolved.

Chapter Three

That evening, Lucy made her way out to the phone shanty at the end of Rebecca's lane. The phone shanty was a small wooden structure that housed a phone the entire Amish community shared.

Lucy's entire body trembled as she shut the door behind her and reached to pull the paper Cody had given her out of her pocket.

Reaching for the phone, Lucy jumped in surprise as it started ringing. Lifting it up to answer it, Lucy said, "Hello?" into the receiver.

"Well, how lucky am I?" A familiar voice spoke back into her ear, "This is Lucy, isn't it?"

Lucy nodded her head to herself, dread filling her heart as she recognized the caller, "Michael. What a surprise."

Michael laughed, "You don't sound too thrilled to hear from me!"

She certainly wasn't. Michael was the last person she wanted to hear from at this time.

"I'm just tired," Lucy heard herself mutter.

"How are things going with your sister?" Michael's voice sounded strained, as if he knew something was wrong but was unsure how to tackle the issue.

"They're fine." Lucy stated dryly, "Just fine. I'm staying very busy. In fact, I'd better get off the phone and back to the house now."

"All right," Michael replied slowly. He was quiet for a minute and then asked, "Are you sure you're okay?"

"I'm fine," Lucy insisted, "Now, I've got to go. Have a gut-night and I'll talk to you later."

With that, she lifted the phone and hung it back up.

Once she had ended the conversation with Michael, she leaned her head against the wooden wall of the building, trying to regain her composure. Lifting the phone back off its base, she slowly dialed the number and waited for Cody to pick up.

Lucy's conversation with Cody had only lasted a few minutes, but it had been long enough to set up a date for the next afternoon. Cody agreed to come pick her up around noon and take her to town to get a hamburger.

Lucy wasn't sure how to break the news to Rebecca so, rather than saying anything, she simply announced she had to go somewhere and slipped out of the house when Cody's car pulled into view. Lucy was twenty-years-old after all – there was no reason for her to feel like she needed to report her every move to her sister.

Hurrying out to the car, she got into the passenger seat. Looking over at Cody's handsome face, she felt her heart leap within her. The passing of time had actually made Cody look better – something that she hadn't imagined was even possible.

"Are you ready for some fun?" Cody asked with a smirk as Lucy fastened her seat belt.

Lucy couldn't hide her smile. After all their years apart, she was ready for anything where Cody was concerned.

That afternoon was one of the most exciting days of Lucy's life. She and Cody picked up hamburgers and went riding around the countryside, talking about their childhood and their good times growing up together.

Lucy found herself feeling a little bit guilty as she realized that she was certainly holding back information that Cody needed to know.

"Cody," Lucy shook her head, unsure how she should break the news to him, "I met a man while I was in Kentucky. A good, Amish man. A man who loves me and who wants me to be his wife. Cody, we're now engaged."

Cody let out what sounded like a deep sigh. Lucy couldn't even stand to look at him. She wondered how heartbroken he was, and what she could do to change things.

"Well," he finally muttered, "I suppose we should do everything possible to enjoy the time we have together."

Although Lucy hated telling Cody about Michael, it did release her from some of her guilt. As always, Cody was so understanding and ready to accept the truth as it was.

"Let's go do something tonight," Cody suggested, "Let's go driving around some of our old favorite spots. It will do you good to see some of the places where we used to go on walks and spend time together."

Lucy felt her face start to get warm. Just the idea of spending more time alone with Cody brought the heat to her face. It felt like she had been transported back in time, and now had the opportunity to do everything her father had snatched away from her.

Nodding slowly, Lucy smiled, "Sure. Sounds like fun!"

Cody smiled back at her and flipped on his turn-signal, indicating that it was time to pull into Rebecca's drive.

Lucy felt her heart immediately drop as Cody pulled the car closer to the house. There, on the front porch of the house, talking with Rebecca's husband was none other than Michael himself.

Lucy closed her eyes and then opened them, hoping that her mind was simply playing tricks on her. Sadly, it was not an illusion. Michael was truly there. She saw him watching her as Cody pulled the car to a stop and reached out to give her a hug.

Although Lucy allowed Cody to hug her, she suddenly felt tense and uncomfortable. Taking a deep breath, she stepped out of Cody's car and started the miserable journey toward her sister's house.

"What are you doing here?" Lucy asked, her voice shaking as she walked up the wooden porch steps to join her fiancé.

Michael's hands were balled into fists and he had a certain fire in his eyes as he watched Cody drive away.

"When you seemed so strange on the phone the other night, I decided to come see you," he explained.

"Oh," Lucy glanced toward the house, hoping no one was listening to their conversation, "It would have been nice if you had let me know you were coming."

"Who was that?" Michael's voice seemed almost wooden, as if he had no emotion.

"Michael," Lucy shook her head as she motioned toward the porch swing, "Ach, can we just sit and talk for a while?"

Michael nodded his head slowly and took a seat on the wooden swing.

Lucy let out a puff of air as she tried to decide how to start.

"When I was a girl," she managed to begin awkwardly, "I lived next door to the Armstrong family. Cody, that man you just saw, is their son. We grew up together and spent so much time with one another...that, as the years passed, our friendship developed into something...more."

Glancing at Michael, she noticed that his eyebrows were raised.

"Do ya mean you fell in love?" Michael managed to ask around an obvious lump in his throat.

Lucy nodded, "We sure did. Cody gave me a ring and we promised each other that we'd one day get married."

"Get married." Michael repeated, his voice sounding somewhat flat.

"Daed realized that something was going on between us," Lucy continued, "So he broke things off. He'd talked about moving to Kentucky for a while and, when he realized that Cody and I loved each other, he chose to tear us apart by moving my family. He told me that Cody wasn't the right type of boy for me and that spending time with him would only destroy me in the end."

"He was right, Lucy. Cody Armstrong is an Englischer. You don't have any part in his world at all."

Although Michael's words irritated Lucy, she chose to push back her feelings of simmering annoyance. Instead, she gave a shrug, "That's what I told myself. I threw myself into living a good Amish lifestyle. I got baptized and joined the church. I met you at a young peoples' gathering and I knew you were the type of man I was supposed to marry."

"Supposed to marry." Michael cocked his head to one side and reached up to run his hand through his brown hair, "I don't know how I like the sound of that."

Lucy found herself absentmindedly playing with the edging of her blue dress sleeve. Taking a deep breath, she muttered, "Michael, I do care about you. But there are things I need to figure out. There are memories from the past...things I need to explore."

Michael took a deep breath, obviously trying to squelch the anger rising inside, "Lucy Miller, there are a lot of things I don't know in life....a lot of things I need to figure out...but, from the moment I first laid eyes on you, I've always known you were the only one I wanted to spend my life with."

Lucy looked down at her black shoes, but she could still feel her boyfriend's eyes staring at her. She wanted so badly to tell Michael that she felt the same way about him, but it simply wasn't true. More than ever, she found herself thinking about Cody, swept away by his charm.

When it became obvious that Michael wasn't going to get an answer, he continued, "Listen here, Lucy, I don't intend to be playing second fiddle to some Englischer who's out to steal my soon-to-be-wife. If this is what you want – if this is what you want to be, then I can't stop you. But I can stop myself from staying in the midst of it. I'm going back home to Kentucky...there's no reason for me to stay here."

Michael's words were painful to hear. Lucy sat in her seat, listening to him, wishing that things could be any other way. Slowly nodding her head, she simply said, "Okay."

With that, Michael started out across the yard and toward his driver's waiting car.

Chapter Four

Lucy spent the rest of the day feeling sick. Although she looked forward to her time spent with Cody that night, she couldn't push away her feelings of guilt and sadness. She felt like she was torturing Michael and turning her back on her entire family.

"Lucy," Rebecca sighed as she sat in her rocking chair, gently soothing baby Jacob to sleep, "Would ya talk to me for a while?" She motioned toward the empty rocker across from her.

Although Lucy generally enjoyed her sister, she didn't like the direction this conversation was likely to head. Sitting down obediently, she braced herself for the worst.

"Ach, Lucy," Rebecca shook her head sadly, "If I'd known this was going to happen, I never would have asked you to come stay here. After all these years, I truly thought things were over between you and Cody."

Lucy took a deep breath and let it out slowly. She didn't know what to say, so she decided to simply keep her mouth shut.

"I've always known you care for him," Rebecca said slowly, "And I understand that. Growing up, he was a good friend...but, Lucy, he's not like one of us. His ways are completely different. Whether you realize it or not, Cody Armstrong is not a gut boy...not even a good English boy. My, Lucy, if you'd only have heard the stories of things that he's done..."

Lucy shook her head. She didn't want to hear Rebecca's words. She didn't want her sister putting even more of a damper on her rekindled romance.

"Rebecca," Lucy spoke slowly, trying to decide on her words carefully, "I know you mean well, but you don't know Cody like I do."

Letting out a slight huff, Rebecca countered, "I think everyone else knows Cody better than you think. You're the one whose mind is clouded by your emotions."

Setting her jaw, Lucy rose to her feet, "I'm sorry, sister, but I don't have to listen to this. Just because I came to help you around your house doesn't mean I have to do everything that you say."

With that, Lucy grabbed a dust rag and started to work polishing the furniture around the house.

By the time night fell, Lucy felt like her entire world was in a blender. On one hand, it seemed that she would die of mixed embarrassment and guilt as she thought about the ways that she was destroying her family. And what about Michael? She had agreed to be Michael's wife. He wanted a good Amish wife...not a wild rebel who was running off with an Englischer. Thoughts like those almost made her cancel her plans entirely.

But then she would think of Cody.

Ach. Whenever she closed her eyes, his handsome face would flash through her mind and she would feel her knees grow weak. She wouldn't give up their time together for anything in the world.

When Cody pulled his shiny blue convertible into Rebecca's driveway, Lucy marched out the house without so much as a goodbye. She knew that her sister saw her leave, but Lucy didn't have the courage to speak to her.

No one was going to ruin her time with Cody.

As she made her way out to his car, Lucy tried to leave all her worries behind her and thoroughly embraced the opportunity to spend time with this man who was so dear to her.

"Lucy," Cody breathed her name slowly as she climbed into his car, "You look amazing tonight."

As she studied his handsome face, Lucy had to smile. He looked so good to her, too!

Cody surprised her by leaning forward and pressing his lips against hers in a sweet kiss.

Pulling away from Rebecca's driveway, Cody led his car down the road.

"Where are we going?" Lucy asked, thinking back to all the places they used to enjoy visiting when they were kids, "I'd love to see the Johnson's barn again."

Cody shook his head, "No, I want to show you some other place."

Turning his car onto an old driveway, he led it back onto a farm. In the distance, Lucy could see an abandoned house.

"Where are we?" Lucy asked, a sudden shiver going down her spine.

Cody smirked, "Don't worry," pointing into the darkness, he added, "Your sister's house is right on the other side of those trees." Opening his car door, he said, "Come on, I've got something to show you."

Lucy reluctantly unfastened her seatbelt and followed him the short distance to the abandoned house.

Stepping into the house, Lucy found herself still overwhelmed by fears. With no lights, the empty building seemed intimidating and almost evil.

"What's the matter?" Cody asked as he studied her face in the dim light that came in through a cracked window, "Are you scared?" He reached out and put his arm around her, pulling Lucy close to himself.

"Cody," Lucy tried to find her voice, but it sounded small echoing off the walls of the large house, "I don't want to be here. I think it's time for us to leave."

Cody laughed, "No, Lucy. This is exactly where you want to be. This is the special place I bring all my girlfriends."

All of his girlfriends? His words suddenly stripped away all of Lucy's warm feelings.

"What is that supposed to mean?" Lucy asked, "Do you mean, you..."

Although Cody laughed again, there was a hint of irritation that Lucy detected, "Come on. You know what that means."

Suddenly, Lucy saw Cody for the man he truly was. He was no longer the sweet school boy she remembered who sent thrills of excitement through her and put the butterflies to dancing in her heart. No, Cody had become a man she didn't know – a man she could never truly love.

"Cody, this isn't right," Lucy insisted, "I want to go home."

"Lucy," Cody shook his head, "What on earth is wrong with you? Don't you get it...this is all we can ever have together." Grabbing her by her face, he turned her to look at him, "Did you expect me to really love you forever and someday marry you so I could become a happy Amish farmer?" Cody laughed scornfully, "No way. You mean nothing to me. You're just a cute girl from the past."

Leaning his face closer to hers, Cody forced a kiss on Lucy's lips. She tried to fight him, but he only held onto her tighter.

Gathering all her courage, Lucy pulled back her hand and slapped him firmly across the face.

"Stop it!" She screamed as he recoiled in pain, jerking away from her, "Stop it now! Get your hands off me and don't you ever touch me again, or I'll scream so loud all the police in the county will come this way!"

Cody looked somewhat taken aback. Obviously, this was not what he expected from the sweet Amish girl he remembered from his childhood. Reaching up to touch his stinging cheek, he jutted out his bottom jaw and exclaimed, "Fine. Get out."

"Gladly," Lucy returned as she turned on her heel and hurried out of the abandoned house. Heading for the words, she started the trip that would lead her back to her sister's home.

She would have been afraid of the pitch black, intimidating area, but she was so angry and upset that she had no room for fear.

Reaching up to wipe at her eyes, Lucy realized that she was sobbing.

Her father had been right about Cody. Daed had known what he was doing all along.

And now, because of her stupidity, she had lost the only man she truly loved...and the only man who had ever really loved her.

"Michael," she whispered his name into the woods, wishing that she could undo all that had happened. If she could only go back in time, she would have avoided Indiana at all costs. But now, it was too late. Michael was gone and with him were all her true hopes for the future.

Chapter Five

By the time that Lucy had reached Rebecca's house, her face was covered in tears. She could only hope that everyone was asleep so that she could go straight to her bedroom and cry alone.

To her disappointment, the white house was obviously wide awake with lanterns set up in all the windows.

On the front porch, Lucy made out the form of Benji sitting on the porch swing.

As she got closer to the house, he stood to his feet and walked toward her.

"Lucy?"

It wasn't the voice of her sister's husband. Instead, it was the familiar voice of Michael. The sound of her name coming from his lips brought new tears to her eyes. He hadn't left yet. He hadn't given up on her.

"Lucy, are you okay?" He asked.

"Michael," Lucy couldn't stop herself from throwing her arms around him like he was her lifeline, "Oh, Michael, I am so sorry!"

Michael looked down at her with eyes that were filled with a pain that was easy to recognize, even in the dim glow of the moon. Taking a deep breath, he huskily whispered, "I decided I needed to talk to you again before I left. When you weren't here, I got so worried about you."

Lucy wrapped him tighter in her hug, "Oh, Michael. I have been such an ignorant, silly girl. I almost let my pleasant memories of the past completely cloud my better judgment. Cody..." She could hardly stand to say his name without gagging, "That man is a monster." Lucy felt a shiver run down her spine as she thought about his intimidating forced kiss.

Pulling back so that she could look up in Michael's face, she managed to whisper, "I want to go home with you tomorrow, Michael. Can you ever forgiven me?"

She watched as something akin to doubt and indecision flashed across her boyfriend's face. He closed his eyes and then slowly opened them. Looking down at Lucy, he smiled gently and whispered, "Lucy...you may have not been sure about me, but I've always known you were the one. It may take a little bit of time for me to get past what has happened here, but I'll always forgive you."

Lucy let him pull her back into his embrace.

This was where she belonged. Michael was truly the man that she loved.

Lucy took a deep breath as she looked out across her family's farm. It was now fall and the crisp autumn leaves crunched beneath her as she made the short trip down to the pond.

As Michael had predicted, it took some time for them to get past the event with Cody. Michaels' faith had been understandably shaken, so Lucy agreed to postpone their wedding for another six months.

While Lucy was sorry for all that had happened, she was glad to finally have the past behind her. For the first time, she was able to forget about Cody and was no longer plagued by any conflicting feelings. She knew that she loved Michael completely and that he loved her.

Having reached the edge of the pond, she took a deep breath and opened her hand to reveal the ring that she had kept hidden in her dresser for so many years.

Glancing down into the blue water, she lifted her hand and gave the ring a furious toss. Lucy watched as it sailed through the air and landed with a plop on the surface of the water. As it sank down into the pond, never to be seen again, Lucy let out a deep breath.

Looking up, she saw Michael turning his buggy into her parents' drive. Ach, she'd better get back to the house. Tomorrow was the day of Lucy and Michael's wedding and there was so much yet to be done.

Lucy smiled as she started the journey back to the house.

She was ready to see what the future held for them both.

Tears of an Amish Widow

Erica Hennig

There were a lot of things in life that Hannah King imagined she'd be. A mother, a wife, possibly even a mentor to young women; a widow was not something she'd imagined for herself.

There was an illness running through the little Plain community. It was something like pneumonia, but the English doctors were having a hard time controlling it as well. Hannah's husband, Joab, was a farmer with a caring heart. He chose to follow the doctor around and help him however he could. Since the illness was contagious, Joab eventually became sick.

Hannah wasn't going to let this illness stay in the community anymore. She made the decision to take Joab to the actual English hospital. Though they were able to keep him alive a little longer, they still could not save Joab. Hannah was crushed, her heart felt as though it had been ripped out of her chest and beaten with a sledgehammer over and over.

How am I going to take care of our little Samuel? How will I live? Who will take care of me?

The oncoming depression wasn't one she could push away with a few good thoughts and a well-placed Bible verse. She desperately tried praying, hoping that the God she served would send a sign that everything would be alright... but nothing came. No signs in the sky, no angels to comfort, and no one to care for her and her little boy.

Ultimately, she knew that the community would take care of her for a time, but she also knew that she would have to pull herself together eventually. Especially if she was going to continue to support her son. He no longer had a father, and Hannah was determined to make sure he had a mother.

Day in and day out, she began to do what she could to care for Samuel. She worked in the local store, and sold things she knitted at the market on the weekends. Hannah would help in the schoolhouse if they let her, and they did until Samuel got to be the age that he could go to school. The community leaders decided having one of the students' parents there would cause a conflict in the community as to why a certain parent was allowed there and none others.

Just as the new school year was around the corner, the school teacher—Miss Schwartz—got married and decided to quit teaching. Hannah didn't understand how the community could let something like that happen. She went on a rampage one day and told the leaders exactly what she thought of them in the little church building where they were meeting.

"How could you leave the children with no one? Who in this community will train our children on the right path? You must have something in place! Surely, you're not that stupid."

She heard a throat clear behind her and saw a handsome, young man standing in the doorway. He smiled as her face flushed with embarrassment.

"Ms. King, this is Michael Fisher," one of the elders said. "He will be the new school teacher. We have decided that you will assist him for the first three weeks of classes, then you must find something else to occupy your time."

"'Occupy my time?' You make teaching sound like a hobby! Isn't investing in the next generation important to you?" Hannah felt a hand on her shoulder and she knew it was the new guy, Michael. Something about his touch calmed her, and her heart instantly ached for the tender touch of a husband again.

"Ms. King," Michael's voice was barely above a whisper. "Let them do what they feel is right. I care about the children just as much as you do. We'll work something out for you."

Hannah relaxed a little, nodded in response, then turned around and walked out of the church. She discovered that the men in that room might not have cared for the children, but the man taking over as school teacher certainly did. And she could get behind a man that was confident in what he was doing. She was going to make the next three weeks the most meaningful yet.

Samuel was so excited for the first day of school that he could hardly contain himself. Hannah walked with him a little earlier than most other students. She wanted to be there early to make a better impression than the first time for Michael.

He probably won't even remember me anyway, she thought to herself. Almost every single girl in the community has made contact with him. I'm sure we've all started to look the same to him. Though Hannah was afraid to admit what exactly that meant, even to herself. She hated lumping herself in with all of the young, unmarried girls in the community, but sometimes she found herself acting just like them. Of course it was only a few years ago that she was unmarried and pining for every guy that walked into her life.

Her train of thought was interrupted by Samuel suddenly dashing off toward the school.

"Samuel, wait!"

Hannah tried to call him back or catch up with him, but he had such a head start that he was in the school building before she had even crested the hill the school was standing on. Michael popped his head out of the door, probably looking for the parents of the small child who had just entered the school an entire hour before school was even to start. As soon as he saw Hannah, he smiled wide.

"Ms. King," he declared instantly.

So much for forgetting who I am, she thought as her face grew warm.

"Mr. Fisher," she spoke politely. "I just want to apologize for the way we met—"

Michael held his hand up. "No need. All is forgiven. And please, call me Michael."

"Hannah." She stuck out her hand for him to shake, but he took it and kissed it lightly instead. Her heart skipped a beat.

"The pleasure is mine," he said as he looked into her eyes. His were a deep green that fit well with the sandy blond hair on his head and tan skin she could see. Hannah thought he looked almost too tan to be a teacher, but decided the first official meeting wasn't the right time to bring that up.

"Samuel and I are here early to help you set up since it's the first day of school," Hannah quickly changed the subject before her mind went any further away from the original reason she was there so early.

Michael turned and walked into the building, ready to have a helper there.

"I'm glad you'll be here for a few weeks. Sometimes the first three weeks are the hardest on a teacher."

"You've taught before?" Samuel sounded surprised. Michael laughed.

"Of course, buddy," Michael bent down to Samuel's level and addressed him directly. "I was a teacher in another community before I came here."

"Why didn't you stay there then?"

"Because I heard there was another town that needed help, and I like a good hero story." Michael winked as Samuel's eyes grew wide.

Hannah laughed at the exchange before telling Samuel to make sure that every desk had pencils.

As the boy ran off, Hannah began to explain to Michael what they had done last year before Michael cut her off with a wave of his hand.

"I do appreciate the input Hannah, but I would like to do something a little different this time. The children don't know me, and I don't know any of them. I don't want to really come down as an overbearing teacher on my first day." Michael winked. Hannah didn't understand that logic, and she certainly didn't appreciate feeling like she was being spoken to condescendingly.

"Excuse me, sir, but I think we should at least address what the children did." Hannah was going to let him have it anyway. "The children come here to learn, not to make friends with the teacher. If you think for one second I'll let you get away with talking to me like that, you have some life choices to reevaluate." Michael's eyebrows shot up, but he didn't say anything.

Hannah continued. "You might think you're some big hot shot coming here on the invitation of the elders, but you're only here because I already have a child and they won't let parents of a child in the school be the teacher. So you can take the smug, entitled attitude and stick it... somewhere!" She turned and walked out of the building, now feeling like a bit of a moron for telling the handsome, new school teacher off. She was only outside a few minutes before Samuel came and got her.

"Mama, don't let Mr. Fisher scare you away," he spoke tenderly to her. "Besides, maybe he can help you become an even better hero." Hannah looked at her son and realized that even though she didn't think very highly of herself, he thought the world of her. And she wasn't going to let him down; not today, and not ever.

"Okay," she consented as she gave Samuel a hug. "Let's go inside and show him how it's done."

The next few week flew by quickly, and the fact that Michael had been making subtle advances wasn't lost on Hannah. She loved the fact that someone was even toying with the idea of courting her. Since it had been almost five years since Joab had passed on, Hannah didn't think any man would ever take a liking to a woman with a child.

There was only a small problem with the whole situation, and Hannah hated to admit it to herself. Abigail Miller had also shown an interest in the young Mr. Fisher. She was by far the prettiest girl in town with her beautiful blonde hair, deep blue eyes and nearly flawless skin. There wasn't much wrong with Abigail, except that if she didn't get her way she tended to have a fit. But with all of the guys in town constantly pining for her, that rarely happened. Until Michael Fisher came along.

Hannah wasn't sure if he was declining young Abigail's advances or simply playing hard to get, but it made Hannah a little nervous. She felt like there might have been something between them, but this was the last day that she would see Michael on a regular basis. Since it wasn't out of the realm of normal things she would do, she had already decided that she would walk Samuel home from school everyday. Especially if that meant she got to see Michael Fisher for a few minutes.

As all of the children were released to go home, Hannah decided to see if she could get an idea of what was going on in his head.

"This is my last day," she picked up a pencil off the floor as if it was the only purpose she had in the world. She looked up at Michael at the front of the room. He simply nodded, his face tight with emotion.

"Are you okay?" Suddenly nothing else mattered. She moved to the front of the room and stood next to him.

"I just hate it that things have to come to an end," he began to cry. Hannah was shocked. She'd never really seen a grown man cry before, and she wasn't sure what to do. She put her hand on his arm.

"How can I help you?"

"You can stay," he chuckled. They both knew that wasn't her decision and she said as much. Michael replied, "That doesn't mean you can't try to get an extension."

"I'm a woman," Hannah shot back. "They are far less likely to listen to me than they are to you. Besides, you're the teacher. You know what you need far better than I do."

"All I need is you."

Hannah froze. Did she just hear him correctly? "What?"

He pulled away. "You're right, I shouldn't have said that. I apologize." He began busying himself with unnecessary papers on the desk.

"Michael." Hannah grabbed his arm and he stopped. He looked at her and their eyes met. Tears were brimming in his eyes. She wanted to hear him say it again. "What did you say?"

"All I need is you." He turned to face her fully. Her heartbeat sped up, but her breathing became shallow. She knew this feeling; Joab used to make her feel this way. But Joab was gone, so she attempted to push all thoughts of her dead husband out of her mind.

Michael looked at her a moment longer, but he must have seen the inner turmoil because he finally said, "No." And he turned and went back to the useless straightening.

"Did I do something wrong?" Hannah's heart hurt a little as she was suddenly treated very coldly. He stopped.

"No, but I need to take this slowly. Not for your sake, but for mine. There's so much I haven't been able to tell you because we've been at school. Let's have dinner tonight. Bring Samuel. The Miller's live right next door and they have a son he can play with."

Hannah knew the Miller's well, especially because Abigail was the one after Michael's heart. This was a good sign though, because it meant that although Abigail was trying, she wasn't doing as well as she might have thought. And she wasn't asked over for dinner like Hannah. She would still be careful not to give in too much to this. There had been too many times already where men thought they wanted Hannah, but they didn't want Samuel. Since the pair were a package deal, there wasn't much option once they realized how serious Hannah was about her son.

I guess we'll find out tonight how he really feels.

As he usually was, Samuel was ecstatic to be spending any time with Mr. Fisher.

"Do we need to bring anything, Mama? I can't imagine that a man would cook anything well." Samuel made a face as he finished his thought. Hannah laughed.

"Samuel, don't be so mean," she playfully scolded him. "Maybe he had all sisters and learned how to cook from them. Maybe he was an only child. I don't know, but you can ask him when we get there."

The ten-minute walk seemed to be the longest walk of their lives. As they got closer, Samuel got more talkative, but Hannah became more quiet. What if he decides he doesn't like me? How will I tell

Samuel? Does he even like Samuel? It seems as though he likes children, but sometimes Samuel is a handful. Maybe we should turn around…

The doubting game was becoming too much. Hannah felt a hand wrap around her hand and looked down to find her son had grasped her and was smiling up at her.

"Remember Mama," Samuel said sweetly. "No matter what this man thinks of you, I still love you." She felt an unchecked tear slide down her cheek. She stopped and scooped the little boy into her arms, as they held each other and cried. When Hannah finally put Samuel down he said, "Besides, Jesus still loves you too. And He's the only man you need that really matters."

Hannah had to keep from crying because they had already rounded the corner onto the street where Michael lived and he was standing in the doorway waiting for them. Hannah began to apologize for keeping him waiting, but he just waved his hand as he usually did when he didn't want to hear excuses.

"Anything you need to say isn't going to make up for the lost time, so let's not waste any more with apologies." He smiled as if to say there was no need to feel bad for anything she did, though she still felt the need to apologize for apologizing before realizing that would have been counterproductive. She stepped over the threshhold behind her son and was surprised to see an almost immaculate house with the smell of roast beef, carrots and potatoes wafting throughout.

"Mama, it doesn't smell this good when you cook!" Samuel seemed to suddenly have no filter. Thankfully, Michael took it gracefully and defended Hannah's honor.

"Now now, that's not what we say to our mother, is it?" He knelt to Samuel's level, ever the teacher. "She cooks for you, doesn't she?"

The little boy nodded.

"You're never hungry, are you?"

He shook his head.

"Do you sleep in a house?"

A nod.

"Do you have decent clothes to wear?"

Another nod.

"How about some nice shoes?"

One more nod for good measure.

"Then you only say nice things about the woman that treats you well."

"Yes sir," Samuel said before Michael nodded and stood.

"Now," he clapped his hands together. "Who's ready for dinner?"

During dinner, Samuel asked every question he said he was going to, from how he knows how to cook to why is his house so clean to why does he teach. Everything seemed to be going really well until suddenly the 5-year-old had a different plan for the interrogation.

"Do you plan on marrying Mama?"

Hannah's face quickly grew warm and she studied the plate in front of her, afraid of what Michael would say. This wasn't supposed to happen!

Without skipping a beat, Michael replied, "Well, that really depends on her. I've already made my decision, but if she keeps pushing me away... then we'll see."

"That would be really stinky. Because Mama really likes you and she's a lot happier with you in her life. In fact, I don't think I've ever seen her this happy. She even sings in her sleep now." Michael laughed at the boy's sudden burst of random facts.

"Oh, does she?" Samuel wasn't even phased.

"Yeah. I think they're songs she used to sing with Papa, but I was a baby when he died, so I only hear stories now. But I think she told me once that was a song she used to sing with him." Samuel shrugged before adding, "Do you have anything for dessert?"

"As a matter of fact I do. Then, you should go play with David Miller next door while you Mama and I talk about grown up stuff."

Samuel seemed to like that idea, so Michael went to get the dessert. Strawberry shortcake with vanilla ice cream.

"Where did you learn how to make ice cream?" Hannah tried to keep the conversation away from their relationship for the time being. She was still reeling from the question of marriage.

"Oh that's simple stuff really... I just went to the English store in town." They all laughed. "More accurately, I have a Mennonite friend who gives me ice cream on a regular basis. It's a treat for me and not one I share with everyone. Tonight, I have two honored guests in my home and I want you both to know that you're special to me."

It was quiet for a few moments, but finally Samuel pushed his chair back and got up from the table without asking.

"I think that was my cue to leave." With that, he walked out the front door and closed it behind him.

"I can't argue with his logic, even if he didn't ask to be excused." Michael looked at Hannah and began his thought. "I've been meaning to tell you this since I met you, but I really do have intentions of marrying you... but like I told Samuel, that is entirely up to you." He sighed and leaned back in his chair. "Would you like to move to the living room? The dishes can wait until later."

Hannah was so enamored by the way Michael's house looked that she couldn't imagine that he was actually fine with leaving dishes unwashed, but she didn't argue because she knew this was a conversation they needed to have.

Once they sat down and were comfortable, Michael continued his thought.

"There is no one in this world who has made me feel more comfortable than you have. From the second I heard how passionate you were about the children until I saw you and Samuel walking up to my house with red eyes from crying, and right up until this moment; there is no one in the world I want in my life more than you and Samuel." He smiled when he said her son's name.

"Who named him?" Michael asked.

"Joab did. He was sick when Samuel was born and said that I was to dedicate him to the Lord just like Hannah did in the Bible."

"Were you having trouble conceiving as well? Actually, I'm sorry—"

Hannah laughed. "No apologies needed, and no we weren't. But he knew from the start that he probably wasn't going to make it. In some ways, it made his passing easier, but in others... it just became harder."

They were quiet for a few minutes before Michael reached out and grabbed Hannah's hand in both of his.

"No matter what anyone says or what anyone does, I will always be here and I will always make my way back to you if you ever feel like we're too far apart."

Hannah had tears in her eyes and she didn't know what to think. The only thing she could manage to get out was, "Why me?"

Michael smiled.

"Because you're everything I've asked God for in a wife, and Samuel is everything I ever wanted in a son."

"What about Abigail Miller? I thought she was interested in you." Hannah simply had to know. She didn't want there to be anymore confusion or dissension between her and the Miller's.

Michael simply shook his head. "She's okay as a person and very beautiful. But she's no Hannah King. You tend to doubt yourself, but you're more beautiful than ten Abigail Millers'. You have beautiful brown hair that reminds me of dark chocolate and rich brown eyes to match. You have cute freckles on your nose that almost seem to contract when you squint your eyes just right... and when you get embarrassed or upset, your face gets really red and it's actually kind of cute." He winked at her.

Despite the tears, she managed to laugh at the last part. She didn't know if she should be rejoicing for herself or praying for Abigail. She loved Abigail like a little sister and would rather have her happy. As if

Michael could suddenly read her mind, he pulled his hands away and gave an exasperated sigh.

"Hannah, Hannah. Why can't you just take the gift that God is giving you? Stop pushing His free love away and stop pushing me away. I'm not usually one to give ultimatums, but if you can't make up your mind, then maybe we shouldn't even try." With that, Michael stood up and went to the kitchen to finish washing the dishes. As he left the living room he called back, "When you're done in there, go ahead and let yourself out. Thank you for coming over."

It was at that moment that Hannah realized she had just potentially thrown her life away. She couldn't move from her spot as much as she didn't want to be there anymore, but she had to do something. So she got down on her knees and just began crying out to the Lord for all of the things she had done to push the people in her life away. She had never done this before, and it was weird to do it in a place that wasn't even familiar, but she knew she needed to do it and she didn't care who could see her.

She didn't know how long she was there for, but when she opened up her eyes and wiped the tears away, she noticed that both Samuel and Michael were on their faces as well, crying and praying along with her. Michael was closest to her, so she put her hand on his back. He began to shake and sob even louder.

When he finally quieted down, she put her mouth down by his ear and whispered, "All I want is you, Michael. I give myself to you."

He breathed a heavy sigh and finally forced himself up. They looked into each other's eyes and knew this was only the beginning of something much deeper than either of them could fathom. He smiled a crooked smile as Samuel sat up with tears still streaming down his face.

"Geez, if you wanted a revival meeting, why didn't you just set one up with the elders?"

Two days later was Sunday, and the town went to church as usual. Michael grabbed Hannah and Samuel on their way out and asked them to stay a few more minutes with him.

"I have something I want to say to the elders and I want you to be there when I do."

"Both of us?" Hannah asked curiously.

"Of course. You come as the whole package." He smiled at them and Samuel couldn't contain his excitement over the mysterious way Michael was acting.

As soon as the last of the churchgoers had left and there were only the elders and the trio, Michael made his move.

"Excuse me, I have something I would like to propose."

The elders looked at him curiously and the preacher said, "Go on."

"I would like for Hannah to be my assistant for the rest of the school year. I know you told her that she couldn't, but the rule that she would be partial to her son is a little silly, since I've seen her in action and she's only more strict on him. These last three weeks have been a huge transition into a position I've never really had before, and Hannah has made everything I've done seem like it was extremely easy."

"We will consider your request, but we can't make any promises," the preacher seemed to be the speaker of the elders today.

"There's also another thing that you might want to consider," Michael seemed to be struggling with this one a little more. He looked at Hannah for just a moment and she nodded, not knowing what he was going to say but showing her support in whatever was about to happen.

"I want to marry her too."

The elders went into a tizzy trying to wrap their heads around this proclamation.

"What? You want to marry a widow?"

"What about children of your own?"

"What about Abigail Miller? Surely she's the better fit."

All of these quick suggestions cut Hannah's heart like a knife, but Michael stopped them all with a wave of his hand.

"My mind's been made up. I love Hannah King and have since I watched her stand up to you almost four weeks ago. And I love Samuel. He's dedicated his life for God's use only and he's everything I always prayed I would have in a son. As for Abigail, God will give her the right man at the right time. I'm not that man, and this is not that time."

The elders simply couldn't believe what they were hearing, but suddenly decided they needed to act right then. They quickly shuffled out of the sanctuary into a back room to discuss, leaving Michael, Hannah, and Samuel alone.

Hannah started to feel those doubts come in again, but this time she stopped them before they could start. *I have a man for the first time in years that loves me like God loves me! How can I ever say no to that kind of love?*

Samuel was starting to get anxious, but Michael wouldn't let him leave, so they began playing a game of tag in the sanctuary. Hannah sat and watched them play, laughing at the way Michael looked, behaving like a 5-year-old.

After almost an hour, the elders finally emerged from the back room. Some of them looked overjoyed and others looked pensive. Hannah wasn't sure if that was a good sign, but she braced her heart for anything.

"Don't." Michael had come up behind her and must have seen her body language. "Don't close your heart. Open it up. Allow yourself to feel. How can you love if you don't let yourself get hurt once in awhile?"

Hannah wasn't sure how to answer that question, but she didn't have the time. Samuel abruptly stopped gallivanting and returned to his place by his mother's side.

The preacher spoke. "We have considered your requests and have but one condition." He looked at the three of them equally. "That you must stay in this town for the rest of your lives and give your lives to serving the children of this community. They need people with big hearts like yours, and this town needs people with new hope to bring a fresh perspective."

"Wait, I have to stay here for the rest of my life?" Samuel asked. "Can't I go home?"

They all laughed as Michael explained he had to stay in the town, not in the church itself. "Ooohhh. Cool!"

Hannah was in shock that they were actually letting this happen. "You're okay with us getting married?"

"God has ordained every man, a wife." The preacher submitted. "And God has ordained every woman, a husband. You have been blessed enough to have been ordained two husbands. The favor of God is on your life, child. We know you won't do anything that would hurt us with it."

Michael pulled her into a hug, as he was still in shock that they said yes. He began to cry into her hair as she cried into his chest. They were going to get to start fresh on everything. And it was the best feeling ever.

Abigail still came to the school everyday to see Michael. Maybe she was hoping she could change his mind, because by now the whole town knew that Michael and Hannah were courting to be married. By the end of that first week, Hannah finally pulled Abigail aside and asked her what was going on.

"I just can't believe that a handsome man like Michael would fall for a widow like you."

Hannah did all she could not to choke the woman out with a bunch of children still around. She wanted to be a good example.

"Well, my dear, I'm sorry that you didn't get your way this time. I guess when it comes to matters of the heart, you're just not the expert."

Abigail huffed, "Who made you the judge on what I'm expert in?"

"Well I know good wife material when I see it, honey. If you want I can help you hone that passion a little better so that people start to take you more seriously. Men like a woman that can really stand up for herself without looking like a 5-year-old."

Abigail looked as if she'd been accosted, but she gathered her composure enough to curtly say, "Maybe I would like that."

Hannah smiled, hoping for only the best in this situation. "Alright then. I'll see you tonight at my house."

"Tonight?"

"Yes. If you want a husband, we must start right away."

"No, I can't do tonight! I have plans."

"With?"

Abigail suddenly looked very flustered. "Someone."

Hannah's eyebrows shot up. "A boy?"

"It's none of your business!" And she picked up the dress from around her heels and marched down the hill.

"What was that all about?" Michael asked as Hannah came back in to finish getting the room ready for tomorrow.

"Abigail's been seeing someone, but she's been coming up here everyday for you. I was nice, but I basically told her she needed to stop."

"I never heard you use those words. It actually sounded as if you were genuinely interested in her life."

Hannah smiled. "It's not like I'm not. I still want to see her do well, even though in her eyes I stole the man she wanted."

Michael stopped what he was doing and pulled her into him. "Hey." He looked deep into her eyes until it felt like he was seeing into her soul.

"No one stole me from anyone. I am my own person and I make my own decisions. Take those thoughts out of your mind right now."

Hannah closed her eyes to clear her head. Suddenly she felt something on her lips. She opened her eyes and saw that Michael was kissing her! She instinctively pulled back and it shocked him.

"What's wrong?"

"Let's... do that again."

This time she was prepared. And it was a glorious kiss with so much emotion and passion behind it. Hannah wasn't sure what had happened last Friday when they were on the floor of his living room, but since then their relationship seemed to be on a fast-track. It was overwhelming at times, but in times like this it felt just right. This was the healing that she needed after Joab died.

As Michael pulled away from Hannah and they looked at each other again, she told him, "Just now was the first time I've thought of Joab in a longing way in a week. Should I feel bad about that?"

Michael shook his head. "The memories of those we loved will always be there, but we have to learn to move on. Thinking of Joab in a longing way meant that even while I was trying to make a move, you were shutting me out. And you did. Now that you've experienced some healing and given a lot of that hurt to God, there's room in your heart to love again."

He suddenly became very serious as he got down on one knee and pulled a small box out of his pocket. He opened it as he spoke to reveal a gold ring with a small diamond set in it.

"With this ring I want you to promise me that you will always be open and vulnerable to me about what's going on. That you will tell me when you're hurting and that you'll tell me when we can rejoice together."

She nodded, too overwhelmed to speak. Her vision became cloudy as he finished his speech.

"As I give you this ring, I promise that I will always protect you and lead you in the ways that God is showing me to take. I promise that I will love and care for Samuel as my own and that he will be my own son... just as you will be my own wife."

Hannah managed to squeak out a "yes" as she threw her arms around her beloved Michael and they cried.

"I love you, my crying widow." They both laughed through the tears as they knew this would certainly not be the last time they cried together.

Their foundation was built solidly on the passion of teaching children and leading each other into the deeper things of God. Hannah knew that this was the best way to start any marriage, and she was blessed to get a second chance to do it all again. This time, she knew it would be for eternity.